How Cancer Saved My Life

and Other Stories

For Joanne,
Who long ago worked so compassionately with cancer patients.

Fondly,
Thelma

Thelma Vaughan Mueller

Wasteland Press
www.wastelandpress.net
Shelbyville, KY USA

How Cancer Saved My Life and Other Stories
by Thelma Vaughan Mueller

First Printing – November 2011
ISBN: 978-1-60047-659-4
Front cover image: Birmingham Botanical Gardens.
Photograph by Author

Printed in the U.S.A.

0 1 2 3 4 5 6 7

TABLE OF CONTENTS

BECAUSE THERE WAS NOBODY ELSE

He awoke to the sound of a violin and piano melody filtering through the too-thin sheet rock wall. Groggy, in the semi-dark, he groped the back of the sofa where he slept, adjusted his eyes to the slender slices of grey light between the window blinds. The music paused, began again. Someone in the next apartment must have left the stereo on.

Half awake, he hopped over hastily-packed boxes, brown garbage bags stuffed with his clothes, to the window. In the dawn half-light he checked his mother's dark blue Mercury Marquis, still safe in the space before the apartment walkway.

Beneath the window, on a beat-up formica table his laptop, his cell phone: fragile connections to his mother, his father. A manila envelope with the terms of his student loan, his pre-registration papers.

Slowly he remembered yesterday's jumbled rush: the movers at the now-sold brick Tudor, keys delivered to the real estate office where his mother worked. The airport where his mother boarded the first leg of her flight to Japan. "I need a vacation," she had said of her prospective visit to his older sister in Kobe, "after the stress of the divorce."

In December after his mother sold the house, she had instructed: "Call your father and tell him you'll be staying with him."

Matt had flinched. His father was probably living with his girlfriend at her place. Later he countered: "Maybe I could take a couple of courses at the University, live in a dormitory?"

"So long as he pays for it."

But of course his father had not paid, had claimed not to have the money. Instead, in last-minute hobbled-together plans his mother arranged his student loan, chose for him this studio apartment in whose parking lot her car might be safer than on campus.

He wandered the few feet into the apartment kitchenette, extracted from a large box on the counter an already-open carton of Cheerios. Shower, shave, change into clean jeans, and find his way nine blocks down to campus for registration.

He had not anticipated starting college this way. He swallowed a handful of cereal, gulped water from the faucet, and headed toward the shower. "Just do it," he admonished himself, unsure as always that he could handle the tasks before him but knowing no other pathway.

He was leaving for his second day of classes when he saw her: braced against the iron railing of the apartment walkway, a slender figure in a pale aqua pantsuit, a fluff of white hair. Her hands were busy in the purple pansies of a window box attached to the iron railing. A four-wheel walker behind her.

He felt his muscles tense, afraid that she might fall. The lock of his apartment door clicked behind him.

She turned. Pale blue eyes in translucent pink skin webbed with fragile lines. “You must be my new neighbor.”

“Yes ma’am.” He took a step forward, ready to catch her should she fall. Why was an old lady living in cheap student housing?

“I’m Lucille Ramsay,” she said. Right hand on the iron railing, her left hand reached deftly behind her to the walker.

“Matt,” he said. “Matt Hargrove.” He felt awkward, hesitant to offer his hand lest it upset her precarious balance. With relief he watched her sink easily onto the seat of her walker. He should say something. “My grandmother’s name was Lucille. They called her Ceil.” His father’s mother, who had taken care of him days until he was five.

This Lucille smiled up at him. “You have a nice car.”

“It’s my Mom’s.” He glanced past the purple and while pansies to her parking space where, instead of a car, were large clay pots of camellias, azaleas. In front of them long wooden boxes covered with evergreen branches. It was the reason his mother had rented this studio apartment for him; less risk of another car scratching the dark blue finish of her Marquis. “It’s parked here while she’s in Japan. I just drive it once a week to keep the battery up.” He shifted the weight of his backpack; he needed to hurry down the hill to class.

“Do you go by the library?”

“Yes’m. It’s the nearest spot where my laptop works.”

She hesitated. “I wonder....could you take a couple of books back there for me? It would save me the expense of a cab.”

“Okay.” Maybe she would keep an eye on the car while he was in class.

In the early evening dark, when he returned to the apartment, he found a plastic bag looped around his doorknob. Four blueberry muffins, still warm. Ravenous. he wolfed them down, glad not to face a soggy pizza from the brick Tudor's emptied-out fridge.

Sitting at the table before his window, struggling to focus on his English assignment, he saw her pushing her walker, a laundry basket balanced across its seat. He thought of the uneven concrete walkway past the side of his apartment, the heavy door of the laundry room, darkness if the overhead light were not on.

He shoved open his door. "Let me carry that for you."

"I usually manage," she demurred, but her gaze was one of wan gratitude as he hefted the laundry basket onto his hip. He followed as she maneuvered her walker over cracks in the concrete. He reached forward around her to open the heavy door. The overhead bare light bulb was on, casting shadows into cobwebbed corners. He set the hamper on a folding table before three empty washing machines.

She should not be there alone. He hurried back to his apartment, grabbed his laundry bag of undershorts, socks and towels, a box of detergent. Feeling in his pocket for quarters, he returned to the laundry room.

Afterwards he helped her pull sheets and towels from a dryer, helped her fold them, walked with her back to her apartment. In the dusk a street light illuminated the pansies on her railing. She reached inside to a light switch; amber lamplight shone from the doorway. She stood aside, waiting for him to enter.

A faint scent of lavender suffused the air. Before him was not the crowded dark domain of the elderly, whose deserted homes his real-estate mother undertook to renovate and sell.

The apartment was a one-bedroom unit, lighter and larger than his own cramped studio. On the wall adjoining his apartment, a well-polished antique walnut secretary. He set the laundry basket on a table beneath the window. Beside the table an elegant chair, roses with a blue needlepoint background.

Before him on the ivory slip-covered sofa, two folded beach towels, azalea and apple green. The colors of his sister's old dorm room at Auburn. In front of the sofa, a footlocker, brightened by travel stickers.

Beyond the kitchenette he glimpsed a small bedroom, a folding wheelchair beside a bed whose comforter had a pattern of yellow jonquils. He turned to leave.

"Can you stay for supper?"

He hesitated. "I don't want to put you to all that trouble."

"Nonsense. I adore cooking and I hate eating alone." She was pulling plastic bags from the freezer. "Perhaps you could take the trash out to the dumpster."

Dinner was beef stew - tender chunks of meat, carrots, onions, potatoes in a rich gravy. Crusty warm rolls. He reminded himself to use decent table manners.

She had switched on an old Sony boom box. Again piano and violin. With a pang he remembered his father, whose stereo had been tuned to a classic music station - Beethoven sonatas while they restored ravaged rooms.

He swallowed the last bit of cherry cobbler. "Nice music," he offered.

Miss Lucille sighed. "I used to teach piano. A long time ago." She brushed a hand across her forehead.

She must be tired. He rose and carried the empty dishes into the kitchenette. "You want me to wash these?"

She nodded. His hands deep in warm suds, he heard her soft question: "Your mother's in Japan?"

"Visiting my sister."

"And your Dad?"

He was silent, not knowing what to say. "They're divorced."

"Oh? That's always difficult."

And suddenly he found himself telling her: about his over-organized, real-estate-selling mother; about his easy-going father. About Re-do, Inc, the side business his mother had started, renovating houses from distress sales. He and his father had cleaned, painted, cut the shrubbery, and when they were done, she sold the house and they moved into another disaster. About how his Dad hated his job, traveling weekdays to distribute cleaning supplies to supermarkets, hated fighting for shelf space, hated coming home weekends to the never-ending tasks of Re-do.

He wiped the counter vigorously with a paper towel. "My mother had a hard time growing up, so she works hard. She says my Dad had it too easy as a kid and takes it too easy now." Too late he realized that he had blurted out too much. Guilt grabbed his gut.

And then Miss Lucille's gentle voice "They certainly managed to raise a fine son."

In the dark of his sofa bed he fell asleep savoring the words: a fine son. No one before had ever said he was a decent kid. And now, a stranger.

The next morning as he dutifully emailed his mother, he could not relinquish Miss Lucille's words. He had intended to report only that her car was safe, that the elderly next door neighbor was home days and could watch it. But then his flying fingers had mentioned taking Miss Lucille's books back to the library, the dinner.

His mother's response was swift. "Do not get sucked in by the old lady who will eat up your time, getting you to run her errands. You have led a sheltered life and are naïve. If you need anything, call your father."

His mother's warning nibbled at his mind as he drove Miss Lucille to Wal-Mart on Wednesday, when he had no classes. He had to keep the battery charged, he told himself, needed to buy supplies for himself, so how could it hurt to take Miss Lucille along? But he did not want to be used.

Behind his own shopping cart with its meager cache of milk, cornflakes, bread and Ramen noodles, he followed her. She leaned on her cart as if it were a walker, piling it full of frozen lasagna, cobblers, cheeses, potato salad, a rotisserie chicken. His mouth watered just watching.

As he hefted heavy plastic bags into the car's trunk, he wondered how she had managed before. Did the taxi driver unload her cart?

"Could we drive through the automatic teller at Regions bank? It's just around the corner."

It was no trouble. His mother's email echoed in his head.

But at the bank, she handed him $30.

He protested.

“Taxi fare” she insisted, putting the folded currency into his glove compartment.

Back at the apartment, after he unloaded the grocery bags, he found her putting potato salad, rotisserie chicken on two plates. The strawberries stood in a colander in the sink. From the microwave she removed steaming baked beans. “You are staying for supper?”

Surely his mother was mistaken!

In the dismal January drizzle, the other students hurrying purposefully past, he felt adrift, unanchored, his days no longer structured by the constant tasks of Re-do. The student newspaper headlined basketball triumphs at the arena. But he had never acquired the warmth of team spirit. During the family’s many moves, he had attended three different high schools. He supposed he might go to games now but the tickets probably cost money.

By the third week, classes, homework assignments, labs left him with expanses of empty time. He managed to find his way to the Work/Study office.

A sharp nosed, skinny woman at a computer demanded his student number. She did not look up. “You’re not eligible. Parental income’s too high.”

He wanted to protest that they were now divorced; he knew his mother had to furnish this information to the Admissions office.

Evenings he was easily lured from his own dank studio to the warm amber light and good smells of Miss Lucille’s. He accepted she wanted him for supper, was lonely and needed someone to talk to. Automatically he undertook those household tasks which he deemed too strenuous for her. With her permission, he scrubbed the bathroom, the kitchen floor, vacuumed; familiar chores for which his muscles ached. Her gratitude warmed him.

After supper, as he sat by the table, too sated to focus on his English book before him, her words fell like raindrops over a background of tapes from the boom box. Memories of her life... He was not certain if her words were meant for him, or only for herself. With his mother he had long ago learned to listen and not to listen.

He was not ordinarily a person interested in other people. But over the evenings his ever-organizing brain sought order among her meandering memories.

Behind the glass panes of the walnut secretary were pictures: an old sepia portrait of an elegant man and woman who had been her Philadelphia-bred parents. In a double frame, two enlarged color snapshots: Gordon, her husband, a smiling, dark-haired man in a khaki forester's uniform. In the other half of the frame, a view out over mountain ridges, "The Place" in the Appalachian foothills of North Alabama. On the shelf below a concert program showed a blond woman with a violin...Maude, who had headed the Music Department at the small college in Leesville.

She talked about living in small mountain towns of the West where Gordon worked. The wreck which had killed Gordon's parents when he was nineteen had left him unable to father children. So she taught piano to children whom she loved as if they were her own. For more than thirty years they had been happy.

And then Gordon, facing retirement, flew to Alabama on a consultant job and fell in love. Not with a person, but a place. Eighty acres atop a mountain ridge, a log cabin. From its great room, centered by a stone fireplace, one looked southeast over pine-forested hills of a state park.

"The Place" had been owned by an Ohio surgeon, who once fancied himself a gentleman dairy-farmer. Until his next passion, a small yacht, drew him seaward. The cows had been long sold, the house empty, wild blackberry brambles overgrew the pasture.

She knew it was impractical, that the twisting mountain road, which hairpinned at their driveway, might in winter become ice-slick. She did not want to leave Colorado, her students, the choir she accompanied.

But Gordon was in love and she loved him. He took his retirement in lump sum to buy "The Place". In a state ravaged by strip mines, there were frequent consultant jobs for a reforesting specialist. At the small college 27 miles distant, she was hired part time to accompany the glee club.

Now, under the lamplight of Miss Lucille's living room, the tape in the boom box fell silent; her voice broke.

"What happened?" Matt asked awkwardly.

"He died," she whispered. "For those two years at The Place he had been so happy, planting camellias, azaleas, flowering trees. It was like a wonderland.

"One afternoon he was digging a hole for a pecan tree. They have deep tap roots. He just keeled over. By the time the medics finally got there, it was too late. And I was alone."

"Why didn't you go back …?"

"I couldn't leave The Place. It was all I had left of him. Maude, who was head of the college Music Department, took over. She got me a fulltime faculty appointment. The tapes, they're from recitals we gave at the college."

Finally, the year of Miss Lucille's retirement, Maude's Alzheimer's grew worse. She needed someone with her all the time. Miss Lucille had taken her to live at The Place. It had been quite confining; she had lost touch with friends and colleagues.

Still Matt did not understand. How had Miss Lucilleended up here?

“Six weeks after Maude’s death, they diagnosed me with cancer. The hospital summoned my niece in Kansas City, because she was legally my next of kin, even though I hadn’t seen her since she was a child.”

The niece took time off from work, from teenage children, to fly down. The surgeon explained that Miss Lucille was too old for the harsh side effects of chemotherapy, that she could not return to The Place but should go into a nursing home.

Guilty that she was causing everyone so much trouble, Miss Lucille signed Power of Attorney over to her niece, who, eager to return home, sold everything: The Place, her car, her piano. With the proceeds the niece purchased her admission to the nursing wing of a plush retirement home. All that would fit into Miss Lucille’s room there were one needlepoint dining room chair and Maude’s walnut secretary.

“I hated that nursing home. I hated being bossed by the attendants. I hated the nurse who wouldn’t tell me what the pills were, only that the doctor had prescribed them.”

Her voice dropped. “And then I knew. They weren‘t trying to treat me, they were just medicating me and waiting for me to die.”

“Weren’t you scared?”

Miss Lucille’s expression tightened with an intensity he had never seen. “No, I was furious. All I wanted to do was get out of there, see if I could find some place that would at least try treatment. When I asked the nursing home manager, she acted like I was a paranoid, crazy old lady."

But she had no money. Social Security and state retirement were paid automatically from her bank account to the nursing home for their monthly fee. Finally she contacted the bank's manager, whose wife had been a music student at the college. He explained there was a window of five days between the deposit of her funds and the automatic draft by the nursing home. "So I called the Cancer Center here at the University for an appointment to see Dr. Blakeney."

She had defied the nursing home, left against medical advice, took a taxi directly to her bank and cleaned out her account. Then a bus to Birmingham. "As soon as Dr. Blakeney agreed to take me as a patient, I rented this apartment because it's near the Cancer Center, the University library and the concert hall." Miss Lucille laughed at the memory. "That first night here, I slept on the floor, on a comforter I'd bought at Wal-Mart."

She'd started chemo the next week. "That's when I was really scared. Of how sick it might make me."

"Were you very sick?"

She smiled. "I didn't get sick at all. The chemo saved my life. It gave me three wonderful years in remission, going to concerts, to book reviews at the library, to the Botanical Gardens. Of course I knew it couldn't last forever." She sighed. "I had to go back on chemo this past December."

That night, before falling to sleep in his narrow sofa bed, he felt a sense of kinship. Miss Lucille had lived here, a stranger, alone, worried about money. Only she had been old. And sick.

The next Wednesday when she asked him to drive her to the Cancer Center, he thought that he would simply take her there and wait in the lobby until she was ready to be driven home. Instead he found himself caught up in hospital procedures.

Under the entrance portico, an attendant held steady a wheelchair into which Matt helped Miss Lucille. The attendant handed him a parking stub, slid under the wheel of the blue Marquis, and sped the car toward the darkened arch of a parking deck.

Inside Matt smelled unfamiliar astringent hospital odors.

“Just wheel your grandmother through that first door” a blond-haired receptionist instructed him. He opened his mouth to protest that he was not her grandson, just a neighbor, but already a nurse beckoned them.

He stood awkwardly behind the wheelchair, uncertain that he should be in the tiny curtained cubicle. A technician in a pink smock deftly unbuttoned Miss Lucille’s blouse and smiled at Matt. “Your grandmother’s such a great patient…“ She patted Miss Lucille on the shoulder and reached for a long needle and plastic vials.

Matt flinched.

“It’s all right, Matt,” he heard Miss Lucille murmur. “This just takes a few minutes.” He averted his eyes, as the technician’s hand, brandishing the upright syringe, moved toward Miss Lucille.

“She has a port” explained the technician, detaching the vial, now a dark crimson full of Miss Lucille’s blood. “The chemo lab’s at the end of the hall to your left.” He breathed shallowly, bracing himself as he pushed the wheelchair down the long, polished corridor.

Nothing on TV had prepared him for the sight inside the chemo lab: two rows of patients in recliners, each covered with a blanket, a tube extending from each patient upward to a plastic bag of fluid which hung from a steel pole.

A pretty nurse, scarcely older than his sister, indicated a straight chair facing Miss Lucille's recliner. "You can stay until she dozes off."

He wanted to run. Instead he obediently sat and watched the nurses in heavy leaded aprons and padded gloves mix chemicals and pour them into the hanging plastic bags.

Over the nurse's hands busily attaching her tube to the plastic bag, Miss Lucille explained to Matt: "This is just a cocktail of meds to relax me, to keep me from getting nauseated."

Matt gulped.

She handed him a $10 bill. "There's a cafeteria on the second floor. I won't finish here until around 4." No, there was nothing she needed. She took a slender book from her purse.

At least the cafeteria was something familiar. After roast beef and mashed potatoes he felt more relaxed, able to watch staff members, in blue and green scrub suits, white jackets, or flowered smocks. It wasn't the chaos of TV scenes. More organized, he noticed with approval. Afterwards he wandered along a glass-enclosed bridge connecting buildings, walked past offices, nursing stations, a chapel.

At 3:45 back at the Cancer Center, he found Miss Lucille woozy in her recliner, but with the suspended plastic bag empty, the tube no longer attached. The pretty young nurse handed him a card "her next appointment", helped her into a wheelchair. A parking valet drove his mother's Marquis, seemingly undamaged, to the portico and lifted Miss Lucille into the car.

At the apartment, she managed to hand him her keys. She clung to her walker as he guided her inside, straight to her bed, uncertain what to do next. "Do you want some soup?"

She shook her head. "Sleep." She was still fully clothed. He pulled off her shoes, placed a beach towel over her and turned on the bedside lamp.

He wondered if he should stay the night on her couch. But after he went home, fixed himself a cheese sandwich, and looked in on her again, he found her sleeping soundly. Through these thin walls he could hear her if she awakened and called out.

"No chemo today," Miss Lucille said on their next Wednesday trip to the Center, "just blood work. I should be finished by two."

More comfortable now that the hospital was familiar, he was pleased by its purposeful routines.

As he waited in the cafeteria line, his eyes strayed along the job openings posted on the wall. RNs. LPNs, lab techs. Then "Linen Supply - night shift 10 pm - 7am. Must be high school graduate or GED. $7.62 per hour". His heart quickened.

All during his chicken pot pie and chocolate popsicle, his mind tugged at the idea. Nights. He could attend morning classes, sleep afternoons. It would work for him. He needed the money. On the way out, he copied the building number for Personnel and set out through the long bridge to building five.

In the anteroom of Personnel stood a row of computers, with a sign "All applicants must fill out computer questionnaire prior to interview."

At first it was easy, until he came to the blank requiring "name and address of parents, if applicant is a minor". He was nineteen, was he still a minor? How could he explain that the only address for his mother was his sister's in Kobe, temporary but no real home, or that his sole connection to his father was a cell phone number?

Then the most daunting requirement of all "List references." His high school math teacher had allowed anyone with a B average to use his name as a reference on college applications. Two colleagues of his mother's who did not really know him had also been listed. But for a job? He shook his head in frustration, got up and slowly made his was back to the Cancer Center.

"You look glum," Miss Lucille commented on the drive home.

He explained the linen supply opening, its feasible hours. He figured she would point out that it was only a laundry job, nothing to be concerned about.

"It's a splendid idea. You'd get to see every department in the hospital, learn whether anything in the medical field interests you."

But his mother planned for him to major in engineering. "They require a work reference. The only place I've ever worked has been Re-do".

The next morning he found two envelopes at his door. In one the now familiar "taxi" money. The other, an ivory envelope, unsealed. Inside, in precise upright script a letter directed to Personnel: "Matthew Hargrove has worked for me as a personal assistant and driver. He is intelligent, highly responsible and energetic. He will be an excellent employee on any job he undertakes. Sincerely yours, Lucille Ramsay, Assistant Professor Emerita, Leesville Community College." He inhaled deeply. Somehow he had to live up to her words.

He began work on Friday night. Saturday morning, over a breakfast of cheese grits, scrambled eggs and apple muffins, Miss Lucille inquired how it had gone.

"I'll make it." Proud and happy inside, knowing that he could.

He liked the order to which work restored his life. He liked coming home from morning classes to lunch at Miss Lucille's, since he now slept through the dinner hour. He liked being off Wednesday and Thursday nights so that he could prepare for his weekly quizzes the last two class days of the week.

The scarlet camellias in Miss Lucille's parking-space garden were followed by yellow jonquils, and then, in the warm air of early spring, Dutch iris.

At spring break his counterpart on the dayshift scheduled a trip to the beach. Matt's supervisor asked him to work four hours overtime each morning, since he had no classes. Time and a half!

Unfortunately Miss Lucille had other plans for his time. "There's a coffee concert this Friday morning," she explained. The Preservation Hall jazz band from New Orleans. I've bought two tickets."

He did not want to go, did not want to lose the morning's overtime. He had never been to a concert, would not know how to act, what to wear. But Miss Lucille paid him well for their Wednesday shopping trips, fed him daily for the small chores he did at her apartment. He did not want to disappoint her.

Dutifully he brushed off his navy blazer, polished his black shoes, and, at the last moment even had his hair cut. On his way home from the hospital he went by the concert hall, examined the driveway at the entrance, the lot across the street where he would park the Marquis.

On Friday morning busloads of old people, mostly old ladies, carefully eased themselves down from buses labeled "Fairhaven" or "St. Martin's Retirement Home". As he pulled up behind them, lifted Miss Lucille's wheelchair out of the trunk and settled her into it, he heard a stranger's querulous voice: "If only MY grandson would take care of me like that."

And the music! He felt Miss Lucille's fingers tapping his arm to the beat. He smiled as one old gentleman pulled his wife up into the aisle and began dancing. The old ladies were bouncing in their seats.

Afterwards they went to a Persian restaurant full of musicians with their instruments, and feasted on shish kabob. "I had fun," he later told Miss Lucille in wonder.

When he arrived back at the apartment at noon on Sunday, he was greeted by her plans for the afternoon. He only managed to get a two hour nap before she directed him on roads arched by white pear blossoms, past budding quince at the iron gates to the Botanical Gardens. He could feel her breathe in the warm spring air, heard her enchanted gasps before a sundial surrounded by red Emperor Tulips. Inside the greenhouse the fragrance of lilies surrounded them.

He reached down and tucked the beach towel securely around her as he wheeled her past rose beds into a small old-fashioned garden. A pink rambler cascaded beside a wooden bench. "It's so lovely," she gasped.

All afternoon he pushed the wheelchair along gravel paths, under the towering red wooden gate to the Japanese gardens, past a carp pool overhung by cherry blossoms. His arms ached from the weight of the wheelchair.

Miss Lucille inhaled deeply. “I never want to leave.”

He was growing impatient. He glanced at his watch: 4:15. “I have to get some sleep before my shift."" But she paused by the fountains, delayed to smell the aroma of tea olive. Annoyed, he felt his needed sleep time squandered.

Back in the car, she was euphoric. “Can we stop at Dino’s for supper?”

“No.”His hand clenched on the steering wheel. The clock on the dashboard blinked 5:14. Three hours to sleep before he left for work.

As he helped her into the door of her apartment, she turned. “Next Sunday, can we drive up to see The Place? I haven’t been there for over three years.” Her voice was wistful.

His mother’s warning: “she’ll eat up all your time.”

“No,” he said firmly, left her and entered his own apartment.
His mother’s email was adamant: “Arriving Delta flight #433, Thursday, April 2, 9:45 am. Pick me up at the airport.” Tomorrow morning: he would miss math class.

When he went next door to fetch Miss Lucille for their weekly shopping, she was lying on the couch.

“Are you feeling bad?”

"No, just a little tired." She indicated a list on the table, her Visa card beside it. "Could you get my groceries for me?"

"Do you want me to call a doctor?"

"No, I'll be fine."

He looked at her, uncertain, summoning memories of patients he passed in the hospital halls. She did not look that sick.

Hurrying from the parking lot into Wal-Mart, he realized that after tomorrow he would no longer have the car. How would he get Miss Lucille's supplies and his?

He raced down the aisles, pushing two carts, one for himself, one for her. He'd better stock up. He looked at her list, longer than usual, as he loaded frozen foods.

Back home, he put away her groceries, microwaved chicken-noodle soup for her, and tried unsuccessfully to decline the $30 taxi money.

"I have to wash the car," he explained, leaving. "My Mom's coming back tomorrow." He did not know if Miss Lucille heard him.

By the time he finished brushing the Marquis out, rinsing and polishing it, the street light had come on. Miss Lucille's window was dark. He headed down to the mathematics building to leave tomorrow's assignment under his instructor's door.

As he loaded her luggage into the trunk, he watched his mother walk around to the driver's side, her dark eyes inspecting the car's finish.

She reached out her hand for the keys. "I'm exhausted," she said. "Eleven hours through too many time zones."

He saw her eyes flicker across the dashboard, checking the mileage. "Do you want me to drive?"

"You don't know where we are going."

They were going, he learned, to a townhouse the agency had offered her. "Six months rent free while Re-do repairs it, then a hefty commission when I sell it."

He noted the plans for Re-do. Were she and his father getting back together? His pulse quickened.

But she did not mention his father as she chattered about Japan, how unsuitable it was for an American girl like Karen. "All the American and European men date Japanese girls. Japanese men are only interested in making connections."

At her real estate office she left her luggage and picked up the keys to the townhouse. Through the drive-through lane at McDonalds, then to the storage facility. At her instruction he loaded cleaning supplies, the vacuum, a small step-ladder. He had forgotten how his mother's hyper-organization disorganized him. 'The whirling dervish' his father had dubbed her behind her back.

The townhouse was in shambles. Weeds grown almost knee high; inside it smelled damp, musty. His mother flicked a light switch and an overhead chandelier revealed the soiled grey carpet. "I told the agency to have the utilities turned on." She strode into the kitchen, turned on a faucet from which water spurted. She placed the McDonalds bag on the counter. "This should hold you until I get back."

"How long…?"

She raked a nervous hand through bronzed hair. "Marilyn said I could crash at her place. I'm beat." She glanced around the living room. "The movers are scheduled to bring the furniture tomorrow afternoon. I hate putting furniture on top of dirt. Do what you can here and in one of the upstairs bedrooms." She headed toward the door.

"I need you to drive me home by nine," he called after her.

It was after ten before she took him back to his apartment. "I'll pick you up at eight tomorrow."

"I have chemistry lab tomorrow morning."

"Don't they give you cuts?"

"No," he lied, and closed the door behind him. Thank goodness it was Thursday night so he didn't have to work.

The movers had left. Sofa, chairs, a table stood around the perimeter of the living room where yesterday he had cleaned the carpet. Beds in two upstairs bedrooms, mold cleaned from the bath.

He was dead tired. And he was facing eight hours of work at the hospital. At least the place smelled better; the heat had taken the chill off.

"You'd better make your bed."

"I have to work tonight."

Afterwards he could not clearly remember how it had started, .remembered only the rage building up in his chest as he had scrubbed the bathroom tile, had stood aside as his mother instructed placement of their too-often-moved furniture.

A torrent of comments by her and he knew: she expected him to move back in with her, resume the tasks of Re-do without his father. "I can't do it, Mom. I have to work

"Nonsense. The semester will be over in four weeks. You'll have the entire summer."

"But my apartment....my job..." - the essence of his newly achieved identity.

Her nostrils quivered. "You mean your job as a laundryman? You won't have to work. Living here you won't have any expenses."

He was not skilled at verbal combat. Finally, listening to her rant about her struggles to build Re-do for him and his ungrateful father, he interrupted. "I have to be at work by ten. I need to look in on Miss Lucille."

Vengeance darkened her face. "I'm you MOTHER. You need to look after ME."

In the end, he had called a cab. The fare cost him Miss Lucille's $30. But he made it to work on time.

It was Saturday evening before he could visit Miss Lucille. "I'm sorry," he apologized, looking around the tidy apartment for undone tasks. "What do you need me to do?"

"Everything's fine," she smiled, sitting up slowly from the couch. 'The Visiting Nurse sent an aide over to tend to me. If you have time, put on a tape so we can we can listen to some music together."

On Wednesday she asked him to ride in the taxi with her to the Cancer Center. In the waiting room he was reading his English assignment when a nurse summoned him.

The doctor behind the desk was heavy set, a furrow between his dark eyebrows. Hesitantly Matt took a chair the nurse had indicated.

"Monica tells me you bring Mrs. Ramsay to her appointments but you're not kin."

"No, sir. A neighbor."

Over a pile of charts Dr. Blankeney peered at him with a hint of a smile. "A very good neighbor." The smile faded. "She needs to be in a nursing home."

Matt nodded, knowing that it was true, knowing that Miss Lucille would hate it.

"Our social worker is checking for a bed at Elmhurst. She's already talked with a legal assistant at Ralston and Ray. They carry Mrs. Ramsay's Power of Attorney."

"Does Miss Lucille ...Mrs. Ramsay...is she okay with this?"

Dr. Blakeney cleared his throat. "She accepts the inevitable." He paused. "You're a student?"

"At the University."

"She wants you to ride with her to the nursing home. Can you do that?"

"Of course."

In the taxi Miss Lucille was silent, unprotesting, but Matt could feel her arm tremble beside him.

The cab pulled into a circular driveway only two blocks from the hospital. Matt exhaled in relief; surely, this near, they could look after her.

The nursing home felt too warm, its air heavy with the smell of antiseptic, urine and a too-sweet floral spray. At the reception desk he relinquished the fat manila envelope he'd brought from the Center. He followed a pink-smocked attendant as she wheeled Miss Lucille down the hall.

"You got to wait outside," the woman informed him, "while I get her in the bed."

"My nightgowns..." Miss Lucille murmured, worry fingering her words.

"He gonna bring your things later, honey. Right now we're going to put you in a hospital gown."

Restless, he walked the hall until the door opened.

Miss Lucille was propped up on pillows. "I'm sorry to be such a bother."

"No problem. What do you need me to bring you?"

She reached over to the bedside table, removed her wallet and keys from her purse and handed them to him. "There's a black carry-on case inside the bedroom closet, already packed."

The attendant interrupted. "Maybe some pictures, stuff from home."

He gazed around the drab room, its tan vinyl recliner, the chest of drawers, a bleach-faded green counterpane. His practiced eye measured wall space for her beloved blue needlepoint chair.

A white-capped nurse came in with a medicine cup and poured water. "This will help you relax."

In Miss Lucille's lavender-scented apartment, the morning's events came tumbling down on him. He had found the carry-on. Beyond that he was uncertain. How long would she be in the nursing home? When would she be coming back here? Who would take care of her plants while she was gone?

The legal assistant at Ralston and Ray was crisp-voiced and matter of fact. Yes, she was handling Mrs. Ramsay's financial obligations. No, there were no plans for her to return to her apartment. The firm was terminating the lease. No, their office did not manage household possessions; that was the responsibility of the family.

Wearily he did not protest. There wasn't any family. Except the niece in Kansas City who had devastated Miss Lucille by putting her in that first nursing home.

He did not know what to do. Finally he found the only Kansas City number in her address book and dialed it. He was unprepared for the outburst following his explanation of Miss Lucille's Elmhurst admission.

"She's needed to be in nursing home for years. I took two weeks off from work, flew down to that miserable North Alabama farm, took care of everything. Three months later I get a call she's left the place against medical advice. Some banker was threatening to sue if they didn't refund her admissions fee." She paused. "What did you say your name was?"

"Matt Hargrove. I live next door."

"You probably mean well, Mr. Hargrove, but don't expect her to leave you anything for your efforts. It's all going, if there's anything she hasn't squandered, to some damned music school."

Exhausted he took the cell phone from his ear, mumbled a hasty 'Thank you' and hung up. It was up to him. There was nobody else.

He looked around the room at the pictures in the glass-fronted secretary, the old Sony boom box, the carefully folded beach towels on the sofa. He reached for a pad and paper from the secretary and began his list.

His heart pounded as his fingers entered the cell phone number. Fearing that the number no longer existed, that if it existed his father would not answer, that if he did answer...

"Hullo. Hargrove here." His father's voice, relaxed and jovial.

"Dad?

"Matt. I been thinking about you. You doing okay?"

Over the sudden lump in his throat. "I'm all right."

"Your Mom said you were going to start college."

He thought of the refused tuition. "Yeah." He forced himself to the task at hand. "Dad, can I borrow your van?" He did not even know where his father was, whether he could get a bus to go pick up the van.

"You moving?"

"No, my neighbor. An elderly lady." He found himself telling his father about Miss Lucille.

And then his father's voice. "I'm working in apartment maintenance here in Center Point. Gimme your address. I should make it over to Southside by six."

Loading the van in easy tandem with his father, he remembered the hours they had worked together on houses his mother sold. His father was like the large teddy bear his grandmother had given him as a toddler.

"You sure she's got room for all this?"

"I don't know." He did not know if this were what she wanted, if it were too much, too little. But when he saw Miss Lucille's face as his father lugged the blue chair into the room, he knew it was okay.

As he watched his father spread the daffodil comforter over Miss Lucille's bed, warm gratitude washed over him.

"You have such a fine son."

His father's gruff response: "He'll do. The other things in your apartment…?"

"Take anything you can use, Matt." She turned her face toward the wall. "Maybe call the Salvation Army to pick up the rest."

He could not bear it. "Your walnut secretary. I'll move it into my apartment until you come home."

Afterwards they went to Wendy's for hamburgers. "She's not coming home, Matt."

Sadly he nodded.

"She has some decent things there. If she wants, I can call Gus, ask him to make an offer". Gus ran the second-hand shop to which Re-do sold discarded furniture from houses they renovated. “You might as well take whatever you can use. Gus won‘t pay much, but your friend probably needs the cash.”

His father pushed his portion of French fries toward Matt. “Florine has me on a diet.”

Matt swallowed. This was the first time his father had mentioned the woman’s name.

“She takes good care of me.” His father leaned back against the red upholstery of the booth. “She wants to get married.”

Matt looked at him questioningly.

“It’s not a bad idea. Only problem is, she’s pregnant. Insists she’s going ahead and have the baby, no matter what.”

“Your baby?”

“No doubt about that.” His father looked down at his large hands. “ I’ve finished raising one family. I don’t know about taking on a kid again.”

Later that night, as Matt inched the walnut secretary from Miss Lucille’s into his apartment, wishing that his father had stayed to help him, he was aware of an emptiness inside him. With his usual ease, his father had slid out of his role as Matt’s parent, had let go of any further responsibility for his son’s well-being.

It was Sunday morning after his shift ended before he could finally visit her. He entered Elmhurst through a side door nearest her room, passed an empty nursing station.

Miss Lucille was lying in bed, eyes closed, her thin frame scarcely forming a bulge under the yellow-flowered quilt. At first he thought she was sleeping. But then her eyes fluttered open. "Matt. You're here."

"I brought you some creamed chicken and a croissant from the deli." Her favorite.

He saw her struggle to rise onto her elbow. He reached down and pressed the button which raised the head of her bed. As she braced against him and he moved her upward onto her pillow, she felt as fragile as a wounded bird.

She reached toward the take-out carton, hands shaking, and then fell back. "I'm afraid I can't."

Only four days since he had left her here. How? He set the carton on the hospital table which swung out over her bed, and peeled the wrapper from a plastic spoon.

It was like feeding a baby bird, he thought, small spoonfuls into her eager open mouth.

His back to the door, he was startled by a grumbling voice behind him. "You trying to strangle her?" An obese woman in a purple and green smock approached the bed. "How'd you get in here? Visiting hours don't start 'til afternoon. Don't you know you're supposed to sign in?"

He saw the light in Miss Lucille's eyes dim. "I didn't know."

"I got to wash her," muttered the attendant, lowering the head of the bed.

He felt his muscles tighten, but a voice inside his head admonished him to cool it lest his anger cause the nurse to take out her resentment on Miss Lucille. "I'm sorry." He forced himself to look at the woman directly and smile. "I won't do it again."

The attendant dumped the take-out carton into a plastic bag extruding from a trash basket. "She's on a special diet."

He held himself steady. "Maybe you could let me have just a few minutes with her to say goodbye."

The woman shrugged, grasped the plastic trash bag, and waddled out.

Miss Lucille's eyes had closed. He couldn't leave her like this. Frantically he looked around the room. Her boom box stood on a chest of drawers across the room. He moved it to her bedside table, plugged it in. A tape began: piano and violin.

"Ravel," Miss Lucille murmured.

He took her hand in his, placed it on the boom box so that she would know she could reach it. "I'll be back," he said, "Wednesday afternoon."

Leaving, he was bewildered by an impulse to brush a kiss across her forehead, which of course he did not do. He had never kissed anyone in his life except under duress.

In his apartment he felt cold despite the warm spring air from an open window. He tried to read his English assignment, got up and watered the pansies in her porch box. He hoped the rental office would not cart off the large urns in her parking space, would not throw away the budding azaleas in them.

Lonely; he gazed around his apartment. She was everywhere, yet nowhere. Her walnut secretary across from the sofa where he slept; the footlocker with its lacquered emblems against the wall beside him. Her microwave atop his refrigerator, apple green and blue cookware on his stove. In his kitchen cabinet the small bowls in which she had served him stews, macaroni and cheese, black-eyed peas. In his freezer her plastic bags of Chinese chicken, vegetable soup, and at the very back a cherry cobbler.

He needed to be able to talk to her, to tell her of his mother's anger, his father's possible new family, the guy who hassled him at work.

But when he went back on Wednesday, he did not tell her any of these things. Instead he told her that when she felt better he would borrow his father's van, drive her up the mountains to The Place she had left, take her to whatever concerts she wished, wheel her in the Botanical Gardens.

She smiled. "You're a good man, Mathew Hargrove."

He had never thought of himself as a man before.

He fell into a pattern of visits sandwiched between his classes, shifts at the hospital, homework assignments: Wednesday afternoons, Friday evenings on his way to work, Sundays when he awoke from his daytime nap.

On Sunday when he asked the nurse if he might wheel Miss Lucille outside into the spring sunshine, the woman stared at him aghast. "She's far too ill". He felt a wave of resentment at the callous words, but somewhere, in a hidden corner of his mind, he knew.

At April's end he saw a vacuum truck outside their building, its long suction hose extending into the open door of her empty apartment. Again a pang of loss. But no one hauled away the large clay urns, the flower boxes beyond them. He took a spray of pink azaleas to her that evening, and then in May, the first gardenia. She seemed too tired to talk. He only sat beside her, his hand on hers, as the music of her past years wrapped around them.

He no longer knew what to say, or even what to think. He knew only that with her, the whirring within him, always driving him futureward, calmed.

On a Friday, the day before final exams were to begin, his carefully organized world crashed down around him.

At noon his father phoned. “Well, Matt, Florine and I finally did it.”

Matt gulped down the last swallow of milk. Did what, he wondered, dreading to know.

“We tied the knot yesterday at City Hall.”

“Oh.”

“Come October and you’ll be a big brother.”

A vacuum inside his lungs.

“You there, Matt?”

He was supposed to say something. Weakly “Congratulations.”

“Florine’s aunt is having some sort of shindig tonight. Florine’s arranged for her cousin to pick you up around six.”

“I can’t,” he protested. “I have to work.”

“Florine’ll get someone to drive you home in time for work.”

Florine the arranger; just like his mother. He wondered what a taxi back to the hospital would cost if the ride did not materialize. “My math final’s tomorrow morning.”

A moment‘s silence on the other end of the line, and then his father’s voice, no longer relaxed. “Look, Matt, I want you to be here. All Florine’s relatives are coming. I want someone from my side of the family.”

He thought of the $42 inside his wallet and wondered if it would be enough for a taxi.

“I need you here, Matt, to wish us well.”

“Yeah. Okay, sure Dad.”

His math book was open on the table before him when the call from his mother came.

“Matt,” she almost purred, “your sister’s home from Kobe.”

He braced himself. “When did she get back?”

“Just last week. She wants us to go to dinner tonight to celebrate.”

To celebrate what, he wondered, their father’s wedding?

“We’ll come by for you around seven.”

“I can’t, Mom. I have to…”

She cut him off. “You’re going somewhere else?”

And then he knew. His father had invited Karen to the party. His mother was now counter-maneuvering.

“I can’t do it, Mom,” he said, hoping his voice would not shake with the rage rising in his chest. “My math final’s tomorrow.” He clicked his cell phone shut.

In the early dusk, he stood in his doorway, dressed in his grey slacks and navy jacket, awaiting Florine’s cousin. Beside him his backpack with his work uniform and shoes. A breeze wafted the scent of gardenias from the parking lot. Miss Lucille. Friday. She would be expecting him.

He punched the number on his cell.

“Elmhurst Nursing, Hattie Mae speaking.”

Relief that it was an attendant he knew. “This is Matthew Hargrove. I need you to tell Mrs. Ramsay that I can’t visit her this evening.”

Silence.

“I usually visit her on Fridays.”

“I remember you, Mr. Hargrove.”

“She might be disappointed. Tell her how sorry I am.”

Hattie Mae’s voice dropped to a whisper. “It won’t matter. Miss Ramsay’s had a little mishap. She won’t know…”

“She fell?”

“Little stroke… but she’s not responding…“

An ache tightened his throat muscles. Miss Lucille, sicker, needing him. He scrawled a note for his front door and almost ran the ten blocks to Elmhurst. Hattie Mae stood by the bed, blood pressure cuff in hand. Miss Lucille lay crumpled in bed, slack-jawed, her mouth agape.

"Miss Lucille, it's me, Matt." The eyes open but unseeing. He picked up her hand, limp.

He glanced at Hattie Mae.

"She don't know you're here."

"Isn't there something we can do?"

"She can't swallow no more. Her mouth gets dry." She indicated a plastic cup of ice water on the bedside stand, a pack of cotton swabs on the tray. "If you wipe her mouth out, real gentle, with cool water, she might be more comfortable."

He sank into the blue needlepoint chair and carefully dipped a swab in the water.

"You got to be careful her head stays sideaways so the water don't run down her throat." Hattie Mae was watching his cautious attempts. "If you gonna be with her awhile, I got to see about a patient down the hall."

As he periodically brushed her lips and mouth with the cool liquid, he muttered "Your lilies are about to bloom. I'll bring one to you tomorrow…" waiting for some sign.

He turned to the bedside table, punched the play button on her boom box. Heavy metal rock blared before he shifted from radio to tape deck. "Mozart," he whispered. Nothing.

He kept listening to every sound in the hall, waiting for the medics, the gurney to take her to the hospital. There was no code blue over Elmhurst's loud speaker, no nurses with a crash cart bursting into the room.

He placed the cup and swab back on the tray and stroked her hand. "You're going to be fine." Unsure if he were saying it for her or for himself.

Hattie Mae finally stuck her head in the door.

"You've called Dr. Blakeney?"

"The supervisor did."

"What does he say?"

Hattie Mae avoided his eyes. "I don't rightly know. Miss Hawkins just said to let her rest."

For over an hour he sat beside her watching the tiny blue vein at her temple, feeling the minutes of his time and her life slip past.

"I have to go to work," he explained over a crescendo in the music. He thought of calling the hospital, telling them it was an emergency. "You've always told me to be responsible about work." Carefully he placed her hand back on the sheet, straightened her pillow. "I'll be back tomorrow." Reluctantly he stood up and headed toward the door. Abruptly he turned back and brushed the translucent skin of her forehead with his lips.

All night as he guided the heavy linen cart along the hospital's corridors, he peered down at every passing gurney, awaiting the one which must bring her from the Emergency Room.

Finally his shift ended. Clutching a sausage biscuit from the vending machine, he hurried toward the mathematics hall. His thumb stroked the cell phone in his pocket, which employees were forbidden to use inside the hospital. But each time he thought of calling, he hesitated.

In the classroom he hastily penciled in every bubble on the answer sheet, flinging it onto a table before the startled proctor. Lungs gasping for air, muscles burning, he retraced the long blocks back to Elmhurst.

From the lobby he saw the open door to her room, her bed, stripped, a black man running a floor polisher.

He turned toward the nursing desk, confronting a white-uniformed woman he did not know. "Mrs. Ramsay," he gasped, "they've taken her to the hospital?"

Then he saw the white plastic bags behind the desk, the pictures and boom box beside them.

"And you are…?" the woman queried.

"Matt. Matt Hargrove. Miss Lucille's neighbor." Staring at the stacked pictures, the boom box, not believing…

The woman looked up from a chart. "Oh, Mr. Hargrove. I have a message for you."

"Miss Lucille…?"

The woman came out from behind the desk and led him to a pair of vinyl chairs. "Why don't you sit here and rest a moment. Would you like a cup of coffee?"

Still standing, he shook his head.

The woman placed her hand on his arm. "We're sorry. Mrs. Ramsay expired around one o'clock this morning."

Deep inside, he had known. He stood by the chair, waiting.

"When we notified her niece, she said that anything from Mrs. Ramsay's belongings, you're welcome to. We're mailing her the pictures. GoodWill can pick up the rest."

He sank into the chair, wanting to shut out her words.

“We also contacted her lawyer’s office. Mrs. Ramsay left things very well-organized.”

“The funeral…?”

The nurse looked blank. “Her remains were donated to the Organ Center.”

His mind cringed.

“Would you like to look through her things before we call GoodWill?”

Like an automaton, he checked the boom box and fished into a plastic bag until his fingers found the carton of tapes. “There was a chair”, he muttered, thinking of the blue needlepoint she had wanted him to keep.

“Mrs. Ramsay was incontinent. It had to be discarded.”

The chair had been there last night, immaculate. The woman was lying.

Numbly he picked up the carton of tapes and the old boom box because it would play the cassettes. “Thank you,” he said and left.

Bone weary, his arms weighted by the boom box, he trudged toward his apartment. She was no longer here. He could no longer talk to her, explain to her his mother‘s real estate coups, his father’s unhappiness: the strong currents which had drowned out the reality of his own experiences, left him feeling like a faint shadow, a vapor.

Defined and come together first in the eyes of Miss Lucille, his reflection in her eyes allowing his disparate parts to meld together. Distinguishable finally to himself as a live individual.

Now gone. Not even a funeral.

Back at his apartment he deposited the boom box, tapes, and his backpack on the table. Not even removing his shoes, he collapsed, face down, on his sofa and slept.

He awoke with a lump at the base of his throat, a sense of foreboding, a reluctance to become fully conscious. And then the memory rose up: Miss Lucille was gone. He forced himself to take a deep breath, open his eyes. The clock was blinking 4:17. For a moment he was uncertain if it were night or day, but then he saw slivers of light through the blinds.

On his table, her tapes. He thought of the college where she used to teach. Surely someone there would remember her. Maybe he could get the cassettes copied, perhaps CDs burned, and mail them to the college.

Despairing, he pushed himself upright, wandered into the kitchenette. He reached into the cabinet, popped open a can of tomato soup, emptied it into a bowl and turned on the microwave. He pulled a carton of Cheerios from the shelf. Out of milk, out of orange juice. He'd have to walk to the grocery store. He crammed a handful of dry cereal into his mouth as the microwave pinged.

After the soup he felt a little better. He picked up his cell phone, dialing his father's number to apologize for last night.

"It's okay," his father reassured him. "Florine's cousin found your note on the door. The party was a mob scene." He and Florine were on their way to Cheaha for the weekend. When they returned, perhaps he could come for supper.

He dialed his mother. "About last night," he began.

“Your sister was very disappointed,” she said.

He flipped the phone shut to break the connection.

After a shower and shave he picked up his hospital uniform to take it to the laundry room. Outside he saw a turquoise Kia parked in his space, a brown-haired girl struggling to lift a large box from its hatchback.

Tossing the soiled uniform back through the open door of his apartment, he called to her. ”Let me help you with that.” He reached for the other corner of the box and the two of them carried it into Miss Lucille’s apartment, now so different.

“I’m Lori,” the girl said, coming up for air. “I’m in nursing school.”

“Matt” he said, as they exited onto the walkway. “Student by day, hospital linen service nights.”

She paused by the railing, its boxes still filled with straggling pansies. “I apologize for being in your parking space.”

“It’s okay,” he said. “I don’t use it.”

“Oh,” she was obviously relieved. “The landlord said he’d have these planters picked up if I called him. But I kind of wanted to keep them, maybe plant petunias for the summer.”

“That would be nice,” he said, looking at her blue eyes, the way brown curls framed her face. Companionably they walked back to the car for another load.

“My roommate and her boyfriend are picking up pizzas. Why don‘t you stay for supper?” She smiled up at him.

She certainly was pretty.

He hesitated a moment. "Well, sure," he said. He thought of the cherry cobbler in the back of his freezer. If he put it in the oven now, it should be ready by supper.

Over his armload of boxes, he could see Lori, bracing the door open for him, waiting.

Miss Lucille, he knew, would be pleased.

THE LAND BETWEEN

I was four when my father left. At first Mama and I didn't realize he had left us. He went to college at night and took care of me days while my mother worked at a bank. Between semesters he went home to visit his own mother in Tennessee. Then he wrote that he had found a job there so he could save money and send for us. So my mother and I kept hoping and waiting.

After he left I missed Daddy terribly. But I missed Mama even more, because after he left she had to take a second job as a waitress to pay the woman I stayed with while she was working. "It's going to be all right, Laura," Mama kept telling me. "Rob's coming back to get us, to take us to Tennessee. It's a beautiful state, with horses."

Every night before going to sleep, I would imagine that Daddy came back. He would lift me up in his arms and say "Punkin, I missed you so much." But somehow, no matter how hard I tried, I couldn't keep my daydream going after I went to sleep. Instead, my night dreams were of falling, falling, into empty space.

When he didn't come home or even call on Christmas, Mama cried. I think I knew then he wouldn't ever be back. But Mama kept on waiting.

By the time I was seven, Mama had saved up enough money for the lawyer. The divorce said Daddy was supposed to pay child support, which he didn't do. The divorce was in Alabama and he lived in Tennessee. The lawyer said my mother would have to file some more papers, but my mother wouldn't do it because it might get Daddy in trouble.

And then, just when we had given up hope, Daddy telephoned. He wanted to see me! The shoe company he worked for was having a convention in Atlanta. He told Mama to put me on an early Greyhound bus and he would pick me up at the bus station.

"You're not going to do that," gasped Aunt Louise, who wasn't a real aunt, but lived downstairs from us. Aunt Louise was a nurse, and since she got off from work at three, I stayed with her and her crippled husband until Mama came home from work.

"Laura's his daughter. He has a right to see her," my mother said softly, a tiny smile on her face. She called my father back and told him she would drive me over and spend the day with a friend of hers in Buckhead. There wasn't any friend in Buckhead, and for two weeks Mama worked nights and weekends to buy both of us new outfits and to rent a car. I think she wanted him to see her, to see how pretty she looked in her new dress, to think she was doing well, so that maybe…

But "maybe" never happened. When my mother drove up beside the parking deck of the Convention Center, my father didn't even ask her to come in or anything. "You can pick Laura up at 5:00," was all he said, as he opened the car door to let me out.

She leaned across to the open door. "Where?" she asked, like she was grasping after him. A taxi was honking behind her car.

My father shoved the car door shut, and shouted "Right here." He put his hand on my shoulder and hurried me toward the entrance. "C'mon, punkin"

My Daddy took me into a big room with long tables in rows, and people sitting at them, like a class. He shoved a piece of paper and a pencil over to me, and whispered that I could draw, but I shouldn't talk.

All during the meeting, I stared up at him. His dark brown hair was cut now, not long like when he was in school. But he still smelled good, like his aftershave which Mama kept on the lavatory, even after he had been gone a long time.

I remembered how much I had missed him. And here he was now, sitting right here beside me. It didn't seem real.

Up in his hotel room after lunch, he gave me a big white teddy bear. He asked if I remembered how much fun we had when I was little.

"Sort of...." I said because I was still mad at him for leaving, and I didn't want him to know.

"Did you miss me?"

I just shrugged because I was afraid I might cry.

He asked me if I knew why he couldn't come to visit me.

I shook my head.

"Joan divorced me. If I came back to Alabama, she could have me put in jail."

"She wouldn't do that." I protested.

"The lawyer said she might."

I looked down, because I really did not understand about the lawyer.

"You know how much I love you?"

It didn't feel right. Here was Daddy, saying all the things I used to dream he would come back and tell me, but it didn't feel right.

"I want you to come and live in Tennessee."

"You want Mama and me to come live with you!" Why wasn't Mama here? Why wasn't he telling her this?

"No, not Joan. Just you."

I was so mixed up, I started crying. He moved the teddy bear onto the floor, and lifted me onto his lap, just like he used to when I was little. Only now it didn't work right because my legs were too long.

"You're too young to understand, but I'll try to explain it to you. You know you're a financial burden to Joan?"

"What's a financial burden?"

"It means your mother is unhappy taking care of you because it costs too much."

Mama wasn't unhappy taking care of me. He was lying. "Mama loves me."

"Joan can't take proper care of you, working. When you come up to Tennessee you can stay with my mother, and I can visit you every day. You can even have a puppy."

I didn't want a puppy. I wanted Mama. I could feel him stroking my hair.

“All you have to do is tell the judge how she leaves you alone.”

“She never leaves me alone.”

“Or maybe about how she slaps you…”

“She doesn’t slap me…”

“Don’t you remember her slapping you when you were little? How upset I’d get?”

I didn’t remember…but maybe…Was that why he got mad and left? By now, I was crying so hard, I couldn’t stop. I sniffled, and tried to swallow, and then it happened. I threw up. All over my new dress.

My father pushed me off his lap onto the sofa, and jumped up to get out of the way of my being sick. “Look here, Laura. You stop that crying and carrying on. I thought you were more grown-up”.

I gulped and managed to stop crying. My father was mad at me.

“Go into the bathroom and take off that dress while I try to clean up the mess.” In the bathroom he gave me a wet washrag. “Wash your face.” He took a towel, ran it under the faucet, and went back toward the sofa. When he returned, I was down to my undershirt and panties. He washed out my dress, hung it over the shower rod, and turned on the bathroom fan.

“I have to get back for the meeting. You lie down in this bed and take a nap.” He turned the sheets down, and I crawled in. “Promise me you won’t leave this room.”

“I promise.”

And he was gone.

When I woke up I didn't know what time it was. I went into the bathroom and washed up. My dress was still damp.

When my father came back, he told me to get dressed, we were late meeting my mother.

In the car, I didn't hug my mother because I was afraid she would feel my damp dress.

"What's wrong?" she asked.

"I threw up."

"How do you feel now?" She took one hand off the steering wheel and reached over to feel my forehead.

"Okay".

I didn't tell her any of what Daddy had said about my being a financial burden. It was like I knew it wasn't the truth, but then I was afraid if I asked... And sometimes, whenever Mama told me I couldn't have something because we couldn't afford it, I remembered...and wondered.

Daddy used to call me sometimes. I never knew when, or even why, but then he would be on the phone, asking me what grade I was in now, asking if I remembered how much he loved me. During these calls he never talked to my mother; he just asked to speak to me and she handed the phone over. Once he sent me a doll, which arrived three days after Christmas, and my mother made me write a thank you note saying how much I liked the doll, even though I didn't play with dolls any more. But sometimes, when the phone rang, I would wait, my insides quivering, hoping, until I heard my mother say "Oh, Louise, it's you."

The year I turned ten, a thick ivory envelope with curlicue writing came, addressed to me. My mother didn't say anything when she handed me the envelope, but she stood there watching while I tore it open. A picture slid out, a picture that looked like a TV ad. The woman had long blond hair, and the man had his arm around her. The man in the picture was my Daddy.

The envelope had fallen on the floor and my Mama picked it up. My mother's voice was shaky as she read me the note inside. It was an invitation to a wedding, only the wedding was already a month ago. Written on the back, in the same curlicue handwriting, was a note signed Cindi, about how happy she and my Daddy were and how much she looked forward to getting to know me.

When my Aunt Louise walked in the door, Mama showed her the invitation.

"Just like Rob," snorted Aunt Louise, who didn't like my father even though she had never met him, "always leaving it to somebody else to tell you when he should do it himself."

"It's all right," Mama murmured. She did not ask me to show Aunt Louise the picture and I didn't offer.

"He's got no business starting another family when he doesn't even take care of his first one."

My mother put the invitation down on the kitchen counter.

"Are you finally going to file them papers so they'll deduct child support from his salary? Before this new wife gets her hands on it?" When Aunt Louise made up her mind, she usually pushed at people until they did what she said.

After she left, I cut the picture in half, and taped the picture of my father inside my school notebook. When my mother saw the other half of the picture in the waste basket, she laughed. This time, she didn't make me write a thank-you note.

The next Tuesday, Mama took a day off and Aunt Louise drove her to the lawyer's office. Later I heard her tell Aunt Louise that a judge had to sign something, then they had to send the papers to Tennessee. It sounded complicated.

For a long time, we didn't hear anything more. A year later, my mother came home late from her Friday night waitress job. She walked into the bedroom we shared with a long envelope in her hand. It was a check from the welfare department. "For November child support," she gasped, "plus an installment on back payments." My mother sounded amazed. "If they keep this up, we can buy a car next summer."

I looked down at the washed-out covers on my twin bed, which didn't even match the other bed. I thought of the pink flowered sheets and comforter at Wal-Mart, and how much I wanted them so I could invite my friend Lulu over to spend the night. "Can we buy the new bedspreads?" I asked.

"Not yet," she said, as if she couldn't believe the check was real. "But maybe…."

On a Saturday morning three weeks later, my father called. "Punkin," he said, like we had been together yesterday, instead of his only sending me a birthday card in the past year, "how would you like to go to the beach over New Years?"

"The beach!" I had never been to the beach.

"Cindi's Dad has rented us a condo near Gulf Shores. We can pick you up on our way down. You can get to know your little brother."

Out of the corner of my eye, I saw my mother had stopped talking to Aunt Louise and was listening. "He wants me to go to the beach!" I was so excited I was practically jumping up and down.

My mother shook her head, "Tell him you'll call back."

"You're not going to let her go," said Aunt Louise, who got bossier by the day.

"We have to think about it." I was so sick of my Mother always saying "We have to think." Like she always made me be polite when Aunt Louis or Uncle Frank bossed me around. "Be quiet, listen, but think for yourself" was her motto.

"But I've never been to the beach," I said, imagining the water, the waves. Every fall at school, when my friends talked about their vacations, I couldn't say anything, because the only thing I did in summer was go to day camp in a park three blocks away. "Please..."

Driving to the grocery store, Aunt Louise kept telling my mother how stupid it would be to let me go. "They probably just want her to baby sit that kid of theirs."

I didn't care if I had to baby sit, I just wanted to see the ocean. If Aunt Louise would just shut up, I could talk my mother into it.

"He's got some trick up his sleeve," Aunt Louise fumed, almost wrecking us as she turned left into the parking lot.

"I don't know" my mother said. "Now that he's paying child support, he has a right to see her. Actually, he's had the right all along. The custody agreement says so."

"If you let her go, you'll regret it". Aunt Louise opened the car door. "Mark my words, you'll regret it."

The beach was even better than I imagined. On TV you can see the blue sky, the little tips of foam on waves as they wash up on the beach. But what you can't know from TV is the fresh smell of salt air, the way the pounding of the surf never stops.

The afternoon we arrived, my father took me straight down to the water while Cindi stayed upstairs with Bobby, who was only one. I pulled off my sneakers, rolled up the legs to my slacks, and ran along the shoreline. Cold water lapped up over my feet, and then receded.

When we got to a gazebo, my father suggested we sit down and rest. He asked if I knew he was paying almost $600 a month in child support.

I just nodded and didn't remind him that it was $400 for child support; the rest was for what he hadn't paid before.

"I always assumed Joan was earning more money than she reported. She's been with that bank for almost twelve years; you'd think she would have been promoted."

I caught his implication that something must be wrong with Mama for not being promoted. "She has to take courses out at Jeff State first. The bank offered to pay her tuition."

"And she hasn't bothered to do it?"

Again I caught a hint of derision in his voice. I didn't explain to him that the classes were at night and on Saturdays, that she didn't have a car to drive way out there. Instead I muttered "She says maybe when I'm in junior high." This conversation was making me uncomfortable. I wanted to go back down to the water.

"She's supposed to be spending that money on you."

Spending that much money on me? I had never even thought about it.

"Well, is she?"

I reached down and picked up a handful of sand, letting it dribble down between my fingers. Most of the time, when I said I wanted something, she told me "There's a difference between wanting and needing." Like this Christmas Mama had said I had to choose between getting stuff for the bedroom, and the T-shirts and pants I needed for this trip. I remembered how last summer Lulu's parents invited me to spend the day at Water World. Mama wouldn't let me go, because we couldn't afford to do anything to pay Lulu back. I didn't answer my father.

"If she's not spending it on you, Punkin, you ought to be mad."

At sunset, we sat on the balcony looking out over the water, and eating the fried chicken, potato salad and brownies from the cooler my mother had packed for us. Afterwards we tossed pieces of garlic bread out into the air, where seagulls swarmed and caught it in their beaks.

Behind us, in the living room, Bobby was asleep in his playpen. Cindi and my Dad were sipping wine, and from my Dad's boom box music blended with the sound of the waves.

After the sun went down, but while the sky was still light, the moon came up. I was so happy, I almost burst.

The next morning, I put on the pink pedal pushers Cindi had given me for a Christmas present. "I would have brought more, but I wasn't certain of your size," she explained. "When you come to Tennessee, we'll have fun picking out new clothes for you."

After breakfast we went for a walk on the beach. Bobby's stroller wouldn't roll in the sand, so my father hoisted him up on his shoulders, while Cindi carried the beach bag and camera. She had just finished taking a picture of Dad and Bobby, and then one of me, when an elderly couple came up.

"Would you like us to take one of the four of you?" the wife asked. Cindi handed the camera to her husband, who took two pictures. "Such a lovely family," the woman commented before they walked on.

"A lovely family." I savored the words as we strolled back toward the condo. No one had ever said I was part of a lovely family before.

After Cindi had changed Bobby and fed him his lunch, he fell asleep in his playpen.

"Cindi and I are going to the Fish Shack for shrimp," my Dad said. "It's your turn to stay here with Bobby."

I didn't tell him my mother never let me stay by myself. Much less take care of anyone else.

"Only if you're comfortable," Cindi added. "He'll nap for about two hours. We'll probably be back before then." And they were gone.

At first I sat there, trying to watch Bobby breathe to make certain he stayed alive. But in a little while I got tired of that and decided it would be okay to look at a catalogue on the table. It was from The Boutique, where Cindi worked.

They came home before Bobby woke up, bringing me shrimp and fries. Then Cindi fished in her purse and handed me $5.00. I looked at her in confusion.

"For baby-sitting," she smiled.

It felt funny. I hadn't really done anything. I could almost hear my Mama saying "Pitch in and do your part." If my mother were here, she'd probably make me give the money back.

After dinner that evening, Cindi showed me how to use her cell phone. "We're just a phone call away," she reassured me as they left for the Karaoke bar. And I earned another $5.00.

The next afternoon Cindi and I stayed down on the beach after my father took Bobby upstairs. She was lying in a beach chair under a beach towel, her eyes closed to the bright sun. I had been searching for shells along the water's edge. I came back to show her a pink one I had found.

She shook her head groggily, opened her eyes. "Oh, Laura." She turned over onto her side, facing me. "I must have been napping." She sat up, and adjusted the beach chair. "I've been so tired."

I curled up on the beach chair beside her.

She sighed. "It's a lot: taking care of Bobby, working. I stay exhausted most of the time."

I didn't say anything, remembering my mother.

"It's not that I don't love Bobby, because I do. But sometimes he's…." She seemed to be struggling to find words.

My father's long ago accusation echoed in my mind. "A financial burden?"

She looked at me, perplexed. "I never had thought of it that way…." She paused. "But I guess money does have a lot to do with it." She explained how when Bobby was two months old, she and my Dad used to leave Bobby at daycare each morning on their way to work at the Mall. The daycare cost half of what she was making and she was miserable leaving him. Then The Boutique offered her an assistant manager job, working afternoons and evenings. She took care of Bobby during the day, drove him to the Mall and picked up my father, who tended to Bobby until they drove back for her at 10. "Your Dad and I almost never see each other."

Like when I was little.

"And then we bought a condo." She brightened somewhat. "At least we put a down payment on it, and were ready to move in when the bank called. They had just found out about your father's child support order. That put our income below their required level. We might not get the condo. We might even lose our deposit." Cindi looked like she might cry.

Somehow I felt guilty, like it was my fault they were not getting their condo.

Cindi bit her lower lip, and tried to smile. "It's such a great place. Three bedrooms, so that when you come up you can have your own room. There's a pool to swim in summers."

I thought of myself visiting them in summer, swimming in the pool. I found myself wishing, along with Cindi, that they could get the condo.

Cindi stood up, folding her beach towel. "Maybe I can find a teenager to babysit Bobby after school. Then Rob could change his hours to afternoon and evening, and we would have mornings together."

On the way up to the condo, Cindi took my hand. I squeezed her hand back. I really liked Cindi. I had not expected to, but I really liked her. She treated me like a grown-up.

The next day was New Year's Eve. We put Bobby's stroller in the back of the car and drove along the beach to a place called "Suds 'n Surf". It was on a long pier that jutted out over the ocean. Way out beyond the pier, one could see the white sand of an island, connected to shore by a tiny spit of land. "It protects the cove," my father explained.

My father ordered me grilled snapper; it was the best fish I had ever eaten. Through the plate glass window I watched the little boats bobbing at the end of the pier, protected by a small island just beyond them.

I heard my father say "Here's to 2011". I turned as he raised his beer glass. "And to spending the New Year together."

Of course we were going to spend New Year's together, I thought. We'd be driving home together tomorrow.

"We're hoping that you might come up to Tennessee and spend some time with us."

I thought happily of next summer's visit, of swimming in their condo pool. No more day camp.

"The condo is in an excellent school district."

I was confused. Surely they weren't planning for me to go to summer school.

And then my father, talking very fast, said that they wanted me to come back to Chattanooga with them, to live with them so that we could be a family. To go to school there.

Cindi chimed in. "We would get the condo and you could have your own room....invite your friends over to spend the night..."

"Mama would never let me do that," I countered.

"It's for your mother we're asking you." My father said that because she had been taking care of me, my Mama had never been able to do any of the things she wanted, or have any life for herself. Like take the bank up on that offer to send her to college and get that promotion.

"My mother wants to do this?" I asked in disbelief.

"She needs to do this, Laura. To have a chance to be happy before it's too late."

My mother wasn't happy? I knew she was in a bad mood sometimes, but unhappy? I looked up at Cindi and Dad.

Cindi reached over and patted my hand. "It's only temporary, honey. Only this semester and perhaps the summer,"

My mother was unhappy because of me?

My father's voice was like a hammer. "So are you going to give your mother this chance, or are you going to be selfish?"

Cindi put her hand on his arm. "Slow down, Rob. Laura needs to get used to the idea."

"No, what she needs to do is to promise me right now. I have to call Harris today."

I didn't know who Harris was, or what he had to do with me.

"Promise?" He looked hard at me.

"I guess so...."

"Good, it's settled." He picked up the check and headed toward the cashier. Cindi busied herself adjusting Bobby's stroller. She did not look at me.

Back at the condo, I headed for the bedroom Bobby and I shared. I flopped down on the bed, not wanting to think about what I had just promised.

Cindi came in and spread a beach towel over me. "Why don't you take a nap, honey? Rob and I will take Bobby down to the beach." The last thing I heard her say, before I fell asleep, was "Rob, you can take your cell phone with you."

When I woke up, Cindi was putting Bobby to bed. She had on a red dress with long dangly earrings. "Your Dad and I are going to a place called Arnold's. Their number is written down beside my cell phone."

Still groggy, I didn't say anything.

"If you get hungry, there are hot dogs and cokes in the fridge. You'll be able to see the fireworks from the balcony."

After they left I checked to make certain Bobby was okay; then I wandered out into the living room. The cell phone was on the coffee table, atop a pad with a telephone number on it. I wandered out onto the balcony. Down on the beach under a halogen light, some teenagers were shooting off roman candles. I went back inside and looked at the clock: 9:30. I thought about last New Year's Eve when Mama, Aunt Louise and I had driven up to the Avenue, where we could see Vulcan and the fireworks there. My mother had brought hot chocolate and popcorn balls. With dread I recalled the promise I'd made my father. I looked at the cell phone. I needed to talk to my Mama.

Cindi had said I could use the cell phone if Bobby woke up and I couldn't manage things. She hadn't told me I could use the cell phone to call Mama.

What could I tell Mama? Should I ask her if she really was unhappy?

I kept staring at the phone, trying not to call her. Then I picked it up. If the call cost money, then Cindi could have the $10 babysitting money back; I wanted to talk to Mama.

Carefully, on the tiny keyboard, I tapped the numbers, and held the phone up to my ear. It was ringing. I waited, but there was no answer. Maybe I hadn't dialed it right. I tried again. Nothing.

By then the fireworks had started. Really loud booms. I went back out on the balcony and watched showers of stars cascade into the ocean. Between rocket bursts, I heard Bobby screaming. I raced back into the bedroom and found him standing up in his crib, clutching the guard rail with one hand, the other over his left ear. Tears were streaming down his face. I raced over, put my arms around him. He hung onto me but just kept screaming. I sat him down in his crib, and both his hands went up over his ears. Suddenly it hit me: the fireworks were hurting his ears. I ran out and slid the balcony door shut, ran back to the bedroom and closed the door behind me, to shut the sound out. But he didn't stop crying.

I tried to think what Cindi might do. "Cookie, Bobby," I whispered. "Cookie…"

The sobs lessened. I headed to the kitchen, his increased wails following me, broke a graham cracker in half, and took it to him. He reached for it, and pushed the whole thing into his mouth. What if he choked on it? I dashed back to the kitchen, found his sippy cup with milk still in it. I took it back to the bedroom, but he pushed the cup away. I got a washcloth and wiped the crumbs off his mouth, but he was still whimpering. He stank. A load in his diapers.

I had never changed a baby, had not even watched Cindi do it. He kept whimpering.

There was a stack of Pampers on the bedside table. He needed changing.

I knew I had to do it. I picked up one of the Pampers, unfolded it, and laid it flat down inside the crib. Then I reached for Bobby, who was squirming like a fish. Finally I got his old diaper off, the clean pad wrapped around him, and stuck the adhesive strips in the wrong spots. I wadded up the dirty diaper, threw it into the john, and pulled the flush lever. The toilet gurgled and struggled, but the diaper did not go down. I flushed again, and finally the diaper swirled away. By the time I washed my hands and got back to Bobby, I was shaking.

I should call Cindi, I thought. I should have called her earlier but I had been afraid to leave Bobby. I got the cell phone, and carefully hit each number she'd written down. No answer. Nothing. I tried again, and this time the cell phone was dark.

I went back in the bedroom, where Bobby was fast asleep. I straightened out the covers on his crib and changed into my pajamas. I went into the living room, sat down on the couch, afraid to turn on the TV for fear I would wake Bobby. Finally I went to bed. Tomorrow I would somehow have to take back my stupid promise.

It was late when I woke up the next morning. Cindi had already moved Bobby to his playpen; she was clearing off breakfast dishes from the table. She put a raspberry pop tart in the toaster and poured a glass of milk for me. "If you hurry, you can get one last morning on the beach while your Dad and I are packing."

The day was grey and cloudy. I sat on a wooden bench staring at the waves, listening to the ocean. My last day here. I took a deep breath of the salt air. Tomorrow I would be home, telling Lulu about the beach.

But my father and Cindi thought I'd be going up to Tennessee with them. In the daytime I felt less worried. When they told my mother what they wanted, she would say "No", and that would be the end of my stupid promise. I felt so much better, I went down to the water's edge and raced the incoming waves as they lapped up onto the beach.

By the time my father finished loading the car, we had to rush to leave by check-out time. We carried a picnic lunch from leftovers down to the gazebo, and afterwards Cindi and Dad walked Bobby so he would be tired enough to sleep during the ride home.

Finally we got started. I knew I had to tell them that I wasn't going to Tennessee until maybe summer vacation. I looked down at my hands, at my white knuckles, and got my courage up. "Dad", I said, surprised that my voice sounded scratchy,"about yesterday....about what I said...."

From the backseat I saw his shoulders stiffen.

"I really don't want to..."

He interrupted me sharply. "Laura, you gave us your word."

"But..."

Cindi interrupted. "Your father's already called the lawyer and our real estate agent."

I sank back into my seat. It really didn't matter, I told myself. My mother would never let me go. I just hoped they wouldn't get mad at me, and not let me visit next summer to swim in their pool.

By the time we passed Montgomery, it had started to rain really hard. Water sheeted down over the windshield. My Dad was leaning forward, hunched over the steering wheel, trying to see the road, driving very slowly. "Maybe" Cindi suggested, "We should pull off at the next exit."

"We can't," said my father, in that determined way. "It'll take us at least four more hours to get to Chattanooga."

"Maybe we should stop in Birmingham. Talk to Joan. Spend the night at a motel."

"Harris said to drive straight through. We'll call Joan after we cross the state line, explain that Bobby is sick and that we have to get Bobby home to the doctor."

They weren't going to stop in Birmingham?

My father kept steering the car along slowly through the thick rain. It was dark now. For a while we followed the red tail light of a truck. But then the truck turned off, and I couldn't see any other cars.

A flash of lightening crackled across the night sky.

"Rob, you have to listen to me. We'll take Laura home, talk with Joan, then go to a motel…." Cindi twisted around to me in the back seat. "What exit do we take from the freeway, honey?"

I had no idea. I was just a kid. I kept staring through the car window, through the rain sheeting down. Finally I saw them:- the lights of St. Vincent's where Aunt Louise worked. "I think," I whispered, "it's the next turn."

At our apartment, my father drove the car up to the front. Cindi got out in the rain and lifted Bobby out of the back seat. I followed her as my father pulled the car away from the entrance toward the parking lot.

Before we got to the top of the stairs, my mother had the front door open. "For goodness sake, come in." she said, stepping aside to let Cindi and Bobby enter. "You're sopping wet."

The apartment smelled like ham baking. In the light, I could see Cindi's damp hair hanging down in her face. Bobby started crying. "Take him into in the bedroom to dry off." My mother indicated the hallway. "There are towels on the night stand."

Cindi looked at my mother weakly. "Thank you," she murmured, before disappearing down the hall.

My father came barging in then, all damp and rumpled.

"Laura, get your father a towel from the closet" my mother ordered. "Terrible weather to try to drive in."

I handed my father a towel. Cindi came out, carefully shutting the bedroom door behind her. "Bobby's asleep." She sank down on the other end of the sofa from my father.

My mother sat a plate of ham sandwiches on the coffee table. "Laura," she said, "bring some napkins."

"You must be exhausted," my mother was saying to Cindi when I brought the napkins. "You're welcome to stay here for the night."

"We can't," my father objected.

Cindi ignored him, speaking instead to my mother. "Could we?" And again, weakly, "Thank you, Joan."

My mother brought in cups and a pot of tea.

Cindi held the tea in both her hands, carefully sipping it. I reached for a ham sandwich. My father pointed to the sofa seat between him and Cindi. "Sit down, Punkin."

My mother's left eyebrow shot up slightly, at his giving me orders in my own home. She sat down in the rocker facing us. "How was the beach?" she asked.

"Fine" said my father curtly. He didn't say anything more. There was a long awkward silence. "Laura has something she wants to tell you."

I didn't want to tell my mother anything right then. I just wanted to be here, to sleep in my own bed. To have my mother kiss me goodnight.

My mother looked at me, waiting. My father held my wrist in a firm grip. "Tell her, Laura."

I looked up at Cindi, but she avoided my eyes.

"Tell me what?" my mother asked.

Reluctantly, I tried to begin. "Dad and Cindi want me to..."

My mother was sitting up straight in her rocker, her eyes fastened on me. "To do what?"

I couldn't say anything.

"Tell them your decision, Laura. You promised."

"What did you promise?"

"That I would go back to Tennessee with them...but..."

"No," said my mother firmly, just as I knew she would.

"It's for Laura's good," said my father. "She'd be in a good school, a safe environment."

"No" repeated my mother, looking at me strangely.

"It's only temporary," Cindi said. "To give you a chance to get on your feet; do things for yourself, go back to school."

My mother looked at me like I'd betrayed her. "Louise said this would happen."

"The judge knows this is a high crime area, Joan. Every time Laura walks home from school you're risking her life."

My mother wasn't even listening to him. "So you promised them, Laura?"

“I knew you wouldn’t let me.” Somehow it came out wrong, like I was angry at my mother for not letting me, instead of my being angry at my Dad.

“My lawyer already has the papers drawn up, Joan. Don’t fight me on this. Any more legal fees could bankrupt us both.”

“It would tear Laura apart,” Cindi added.

I sat hunched between them, unable to move.

“So it’s all decided,” my mother muttered, looking at me blankly. She picked up her cup and saucer and headed toward the kitchen, the cup rattling in its saucer.

No one said anything.

My mother smiled a funny smile at us. “Laura, go get your pajamas out of the bedroom so your father and Cindi can go to bed.” She opened the door to the linen closet and laid a sheet and blanket on the arm of the sofa. “You can sleep here.” She walked toward the front door. “I’m spending the night downstairs with Louise and Frank.”

I jumped up, relieved to be out from between Dad and Cindi. My mother had her hand on the doorknob as I headed for the bedroom. “I hope,” my mother said, sliding out the door, “All of you sleep well.”

When I turned on the light in the bedroom, I saw them: the pink ruffled curtains, the rose-flowered bedspreads, the towels with rose appliques. And there, on the bed I slept in, was Bobby, pooping on my new bedspread without even a towel underneath him.

Furious I snatched a pair of pajamas from the drawer, and went in the bathroom to change.

Out in the living room, I heard Cindi. “Please, Rob. I‘m so tired, I just want sleep.” She sounded like she was crying. I started out of the bathroom, only to have Cindi brush past, my father following. He shut the bedroom door behind them.

In the living room the ham sandwiches were still on the coffee table. I picked the plate up, took it into the kitchen and covered it with saran wrap. Any moment now. I thought, Mama will bring Aunt Louise up here. Aunt Louise will go charging into the bedroom and scream at my father that if he tries to take me away, she will call the police. And I will run into my Mama’s arms.

I lay down on the sofa, listening for Aunt Louise and Mama’s footsteps on the stairs. I kept waiting, and listening until finally I fell asleep...into dreams of the ocean roaring beneath a condo balcony. The sounds of a storm blended with the roar of the ocean; rain beat down. Somehow I was out on the balcony, searching frantically across the dark waters for that island protecting the tiny boats. Then lightening flashed, and I saw the island growing smaller, covered by waves, and very, very far from shore.

LOSS

The moment she pulled her jewelry box from its hiding place, Clare knew. Empty. The diamond and sapphire rings, the cameo pin, her pearl necklace. All from her own mother. Everything gone. Lungs airless, as though the breath had been sucked from her, her arthritic hands fumbled among the sweaters.

The box's clasp had been closed; its contents could not have spilled out. She tried to remember when she had last opened the box: three weeks ago, putting her pearls back after the birthday dinner. Had she done something stupid, let the jewelry slide from her hand? Was it now buried in another drawer? She began pulling lingerie from the drawer below, dumping gloves and scarves on the bed. Where? She hated herself for her own stupidity. Where?

Against her will, the honey brown features, the corn-braided hair, Lurlene's gently smiling face intruded into her mind. Lurlene. Lurlene, who came each afternoon after her cleaning shift to accompany Clare on her walker down to the rose garden, into the cool shade of the gazebo.

She flinched at where her thoughts were taking her. It could not be. Lurlene cared about her. Clare had been grateful to whatever gods might be for sending Lurlene into her life, for giving her this last chance perhaps to have meaning in another human's life.

She stared at the empty case. "It doesn't matter," she tried to soothe herself. The jewelry was insured, albeit with a hefty deductible. Insured against theft, not against her forgetfulness. She dreaded the hassle of an insurance investigator, the questions, the embarrassment if she later discovered the rings in some forgotten hiding place. It did not matter. The rings could no longer fit over her enlarged knuckles. She had plenty of money, could buy replacements for the pearls if she wanted to. She sighed. An insurance investigator might suspect Lurlene.

Disconsolate she wandered out of her small bedroom and sank into her living room recliner. From there she could see her balcony, recently filled with pink hibiscus, fuchsia geraniums, hanging baskets of ivy. All because of Lurlene.

She thought back to three months earlier, when Lurlene had come into her life.

Clare had been at The Oaks for over a year: at 83 waiting out her days. Despite the people around her, the childish craft lessons, the hollow festivities, she had ached- at the base of her throat with an empty loneliness.

She should be grateful, she knew. After a lifetime of frugality and careful investment, she was safe financially. Money buffered her, allowed her to live in this pleasant retirement center, to invite former students and colleagues to lunch in the light, cheerful dining room. But the students and colleagues had begun to visit less often, their occasional emails full of events from their own busy lives. She was careful never to voice the ache, the lonely longing. Hearing such would make others uncomfortable, fearful lest there be future demands, and she did not want to lose whatever fragile contacts might still be available to her.

Her only relative, a great-nephew in Oklahoma, carried her Power of Attorney. Every six months she mailed him data from her meticulously maintained ledger, along with a check for the privilege of listing him on hospital admission forms, in bank contacts.

In the Oaks dining room, she feigned interest in her tablemates' maladies and their grandchildren. Skillfully she eluded weekly visits from the kindergartners, those cesspools of childhood germs whose proud mothers pushed them to inflict feigned affection on elderly strangers. She endured Sunday afternoon recitals of untalented pianists, and submitted to her tablemate Julia's daily demands that she serve as a fourth at bridge. Despite the abrasion of too many people, she felt isolated.

Until Lurlene had slipped into her empty life.

The knock at her door had been hesitant. When she opened the door, a pretty black girl, looking almost as young as the students Clare had taught.

"I'm Lurlene."The girl's slender frame seemed almost lost within the blue housekeepers uniform. "Miss Hannah, down at the desk, say they worried about you. Walking all the way down to the gardens. Afraid you might fall."

Clare's muscles tensed. She would not fall. On her four-wheel walker, she had sense enough to be careful. A moment's panic, lest the administrators forbid her this one last pleasure. "Come in."

Deftly the girl adjusted the blinds, blocking the sun's glare while letting sunlight filter through. "They say you by yourself. Nobody to look after you."

Clare peered at the girl: high cheekbones in a warm, honey-brown skin, dark almond-shaped eyes, bronze-tipped cornbraids. “I really don’t need anyone.”

“It’d just be for two hours every afternoon. When I get off from my shift.” Standing there before her, the child looked so very vulnerable. “Your housekeeper don’t come but once a week. I can do whatever you need in between.”

Clare thought of the sharp twinges in her shoulder when she hung up her clothes or when she put her breakfast dishes in the overhead cabinet. She looked around the large living room with its blue Chinese rug. The silver candelabra on her marble-topped antique table needed polishing. Her empty, unswept balcony. She was so tired.

Hesitantly the girl mumbled “I charge $12 an hour.”

Highway robbery, Clare thought, but it was the going rate for private aides here. And she had the money. “Why don’t you,” she suggested gently, “let me think about it. If you can come by on Thursday, I’ll let you know.”

She had been cautious. Over the bridge table, she queried Julia and Mary Alys, on whose hall Lurlene was housekeeper.

“Top cleaner’” snorted Julia. “Pretties things up on the surface, but doesn’t bother with deep cleaning.” She pushed the deck of cards in Mary Alys’ direction. “I’ve asked Housekeeping to assign me Mabel instead, but they haven’t done it.”

“She probably,” inserted Mary Alys hesitantly, “needs the money. There’s a two-year-old, Mitylene.”

“And a boyfriend, Clarence, who drives a beat-up Chevy with a broken muffler. Administration is probably sick of her loafing on the residents' veranda every afternoon until after five, when he honks his horn."

Mary Alys looked as if she wanted to say something.

"Just deal, Mary Alys." Julia drummed her fingers. "Don't get snookered, Clare."

On Thursday afternoon the girl appeared, bearing gifts. A large red camellia, probably filched from the Center's shrubbery, whose blooms residents were forbidden to pick. A spray canister whose lavender fragrance suffused the room.

Over a water-filled bud vase, the girl stared at a picture of Clare's mother. Dutifully hung to let her mother's memory live, looking down in disapproval. "That your Mama?"

Clare nodded.

"Lots of people would say she real pretty."

Clare felt the girl watching her.

"You favor her?"

"I took after my father."

Again the girl's voice was hesitant, tentative, "Sometime people that pretty don't bother being nice."

Relief washed through Clare. Gratitude. This child understood. For the first time in Clare's long 83 years, someone had seen through her mother's façade, perhaps even sensed the transgressions against her own soul.

The telephone interrupted. "No, Julia," she said. "No, I can't play bridge this afternoon. Lurlene and I are going down to the gardens."

The next morning when Clare awoke to the television news, her eyes fell first on the camellia. With anticipation she thought of Lurlene's afternoon arrival. Reaching over to her night table, she pressed the spray button on the lavender canister. Nothing. It was empty.

In the garden Clare wandered among pansies and jonquils, peering down for signs of new growth. She longed for the plants and flowering shrubs of her relinquished condo, for the dawns when she had awakened full of hope for what gifts awaited her. In early morning sunlight she would inspect the swollen branches of her cherry tree, the buds on her gardenia bush. And then, at summer's peak, the magnificent Asian lilies, her silent offering to a too-often-destructive world.

The routine of the garden's demands - to plan, to plant, to tend - almost as if the blooms were her children - had lured her futureward through the seasons.

Now, resting in The Oaks gazebo, Clare watched Lurlene, twenty feet away, who chattered on her cell phone. Back when she still drove, Clare had contemplated buying a cell phone herself, but the monthly fees seemed an unnecessary extravagance. She wondered how Lurlene could so casually talk away such expensive minutes.

As Julia had said, Lurlene liked to make things pretty. She pulled Clare's embroidered Chinese satin bedspread from its zippered plastic cover.

"That one's just for visitors," admonished Clare. "It has to be dry-cleaned."

Lurlene shook her head. "Why you so stingy with yourself? You got money." She let the yellow satin fall from her hands onto the bed. "My Mama always say 'Don't live cheap'."

Not ready to debate the lessons of a Depression childhood, Clare changed the subject. "Does your Mama take care of Mitylene while you work?"

Sadness crossed Lurlene's face. "My Mama ain't never seen Mitylene. She's gone. To Cincinnati"

Clare wandered into the living room toward her recliner. Lurlene followed. "How long has she lived in Cincinnati?"

Lurlene sank onto the sofa opposite. "Since I was pregnant."

"You were living with Mitylene's father when she left?"

"No." Lurlene's voice was numb, listless. "He was long gone before she left."

But Lurlene was a child herself. "Where do you and Mitylene live?"

"We stay with my auntie."

Clare was relieved. "Your mother's sister. Your mother left you with her sister."

"My auntie's too old to be my Mama's sister. Cousin, I guess "

The child didn't even know. Left alone, pregnant. Clare did not respond. How could any mother....?

Sensing the unspoken accusation, Lurlene lashed out. "My Mama loves me. She raised me." Her voice sank to a scarcely audible whisper, "She just don't love Mitylene."

Clare knew she was becoming too concerned about the girl, her days too focused upon Lurlene's afternoon arrival. When she passed Lurlene at lunchtime, a bag of potato chips in hand, a Pepsi clattering out of the machine, she worried. No wonder the child was so thin.

That afternoon when Lurlene arrived, Clare already had peanut butter sandwiches made, vegetable juice poured. "The doctor," she lied, "says I need an afternoon snack. But I hate to eat alone." Tomorrow morning, she thought, when the van drove Oaks residents for their weekly trip to Publix, she would buy a quart of chocolate milk. The girl probably did not get enough calcium.

In early April, on their walk down to the gardens, Clare stopped in the parking lot beside her blue Camry. Bent over, affixing the renewal sticker to the license plate, she heard the eagerness in Lurlene's voice. "That your car?"

Instinctively she countered, "I don't drive anymore." Her cardiologist had not forbidden it, just tactfully suggested she stop for awhile. She should have sold the car but she hung onto a vain hope that someday she might again drive to her book club, attend coffee concerts of the symphony.

"You got a car and you don't even drive it?"

This was not entirely true. Every Sunday morning, when traffic was at its lowest, she cautiously drove four times around the block to keep the car's battery charged.

"I can drive you and me places. Wherever we need to go, I can drive us."

"You know how to drive?"

"Clarence taught me, after he got shot in the leg." Lurlene was trying to open the car's locked door.

It was a bad idea. But each morning, when the sun rose on her empty balcony, Clare longed for the hanging baskets, the potted begonias, of Sullivan's nursery where the Oaks van did not go.

By the following week Clare's longing overcame her judgment. "You do have a license?"

"You think I 'm too dumb to pass that test? Have a policeman putting me in jail?"

All the way to the nursery Clare's hand gripped the car handle, her right foot pressing down against the floorboard on the passenger's side. But they made it. Into a wonderland of blooms, the earthy smell of plants being misted. They loaded the car with pink hibiscus, South American impatiens, hanging baskets of ivy.

While they were shopping another car had pulled in behind the Camry. It would take some skillful backing to get around it. Instead Clare felt Lurlene shift into forward, full gas straight ahead, bumping across the concrete barrier. She heard the underside of the car scrape as Lurlene headed toward the curb instead of the exit. "Stop," she managed to gasp. "Brakes, Lurlene, brakes!'

The moment the car halted she demanded: "Change places and let me drive." Once under the steering wheel she maneuvered back and forth over the sidewalk between the parking barrier and the curb, until she was able to reach the exit.

On the trip home, beside a lackadaisical Lurlene in the passenger seat, she was amazed at how easily she drove.

At least I got the flowers, she thought, surprisingly pleased with the afternoon's adventure.

Back from their afternoon walk to the ice cream parlor, Lurlene was uncharacteristically helpful. "You want me to water your flowers?" she offered as she hung up Clare's jacket.

"Isn't it time for Clarence to pick you up?"

Lurlene fluffed a sofa pillow. "I got to take your car tonight. Bring it back tomorrow afternoon."

Clare was caught off guard. "What for?"

"Got to take my auntie to the doctor."

"Why can't Clarence take her?"

Petulantly, "she ain't Clarence' auntie."

She's not my auntie either, Clare thought, outraged at the brazen audacity of the demand. "I don't lend my car."

"How I going to get my auntie to the doctor?"

"Why can't you take her on the bus?"

"My auntie got high blood, high sugar. Her bones hurt. She can't be pulling herself up on no bus." Lurlene's lower lip jutted out determinedly.

Silence.

"You ain't even using that car. You get sick, they takes you to the doctor in a van. You need something, people here do everything for you." Lurlene's voice mounted piteously. "My auntie don't have nobody but me. And here you wanting her with her high blood to walk to the bus stop, cause you happy to have that car just sitting there parked. Doing nothing for nobody." She began to cry.

In the end, shaking with rage and guilt, Clare gave in. With a sense of foreboding she handed over her keys.

It was almost lunchtime the next day when Lurlene phoned. "Your car don't run. You got to call somebody to come get it."

"You've had a wreck?"

"Ain't had no wreck. Ain't done nothing to it." Lurlene's voice rose to a high-pitched wail. "It just don't go."

Lurlene's aunt, Clare thought. Trapped in a hot car in this midday heat. "Where in the Medical Center are you?"

"Ain't at the Medical Center."

"Then where?"

Lurlene's voice was scarcely audible. "At the Mall. Front of the donut shop."

Clare phoned the Shell station a block down from The Oaks. Its manager, Albert, catered to crises of the elderly residents whose cars his wrecker extracted from their numerous mishaps. "Might be the battery," Albert opined. "Won't know until I take a look at it."

"I need to go with you." Ten minutes later, leaving her walker in The Oaks lobby, Clare hoisted herself up into the cab of Albert's service truck. At the mall she spotted her car parked at an awkward angle but otherwise intact.

"You stay in the air-conditioned cab while I check it out," Albert instructed.

A wilted Lurlene slowly walked up to the truck, carrying a red and white box. "I bought you some donuts," she mumbled.

"Where's your aunt?"

Lurlene's eyes shifted warily. "Home." And then, as if on inspiration, "She wanting some donuts."

Exasperated Clare did not invite Lurlene up into the truck.

Albert strode back from the car. "You're in luck. Somebody's had the air-conditioning on high, the radio playing while the car was parked. Dead battery. I'll jump it off, then someone has to drive it back to the station for recharging."

"I'd better drive it myself." Clare opened the cab door, sliding down from her high perch to the pavement. Lurlene followed, opening the Camry's passenger door to get in.

"No," said Clare firmly.

"How I gonna get home?"

"Call Clarence."

"He ain't at work today."

"Then take the bus." Carefully Clare edged the car out of the parking space, listening lest the engine die. In the side mirror, she glimpsed Lurlene standing forlorn, her arms cradling the donut box.

By the time she finally arrived back at her apartment, Clare was shaking. She could hear her blood pressure thudding in her ears. She sank into her recliner, breathed carefully, and tried to let go of the rage ravaging her.

This can't go on, she told herself. She dreaded the ordeal of telling the girl, of dealing with her probable persistent protest. Perhaps she could leave a note for Lurlene at the desk, stating her services were no longer needed, enclosing her pay for the week. Her pay. What was the child going to do without this weekly addition to her meager income? Pay she probably depended on for Mitylene, for food.

Having missed lunch she wandered into the kitchenette, taking from the fridge the carton of chicken salad she had purchased yesterday for their afternoon snack. There would no longer be shared snacks, no longer afternoon outings to focus her otherwise empty days. She wondered if Lurlene had at least learned from her to eat decently, to get enough protein.

Sadly she placed the unopened carton back into the refrigerator, on the counter sat the painted watering can. Her flowers needed water. Lurlene would not be here to water them.

She was almost relieved the next afternoon when, without knocking, Lurlene slid into her apartment.

"What you wanting us to do this afternoon?" Lurlene's eyes swept over the empty kitchen counter where their afternoon sandwiches usually waited.

Clare forced herself to be firm. "You can fix me a chicken salad sandwich and a cup of tea."

The girl turned toward the kitchenette. "It alright to fix myself one too?"

Clare shrugged. "Whatever." She watched. For a change Lurlene took the rinsed breakfast dishes from the rack and replaced them in the cabinet. When she brought Clare's sandwich she did not, as had been her habit, flop down on the sofa to eat hers, but left it on the counter as she filled the watering can.

It just might work, Clare decided. If I can just provide enough structure.

Later that week, as Clare carefully avoided any outings that required the car, Lurlene asked appeasingly, "You play bridge with Miss Julia?"

"No, but I see her everyday at lunch." Indeed Julia had been her usual malevolent self today, gleefully recounting her latest tale of another resident's stupidity. "Deserved it," Julia snorted. "Left her purse right there on the table, didn't even lock her door while she was in the laundry room."

Clare had paid no more attention to Julia than she had last week when Margaret, who made weekend trips to a plush gambling resort, complained that her sizeable winning were missing.

"Shouldn't gamble," proclaimed Julia, spearing an asparagus stalk with her fork.

But now, sitting in her recliner, staring out over her flower-decked balcony, her own rings gone, she knew. Had known. She sucked in a lungful of air.

At lunch Clare said little and ate less.

"Is something wrong?" asked Margaret.

"No, nothing. Everything's fine." Carefully she stood and maneuvered her walker to the elevator, back to her apartment.

She should call the insurance company. She sat without moving, gripped by inertia.

She was not surprised when Steve Hammond, the director, knocked at her door, a clipboard with a sheaf of papers in hand. “We‘re having some difficulties here at The Oaks.” Inside her apartment he explained, “Some of our residents have been missing money, valuables.”

Clare could feel her heart pounding, as if she herself were the culprit.

“We‘ve picked up a pattern, but nothing anyone can prove. Have you missed anything recently?”

She hesitated, caught. “Just this morning. I thought I had lost …misplaced…some jewelry. It‘s probably around here.”

He was reading from the clipboard. “Pearl necklace, two rings, cameo pin, diamond watch…”

“No,” she protested, “no diamond watch. I mean, the diamond watch isn’t mine.”

“But the rest are? Hannah, down at the desk, thought she remembered you’re wearing a handsome cameo pin.”

“My mother’s. You’ve found them?”

“No, what we found was a pawn ticket, when security searched the locker of the housekeeper for residents who complained of losses.”

“A pawn ticket?”

“As I said, it’s a delicate situation. We need to dismiss the thief to protect other residents. But firing a black without cause can get The Oaks sued for discrimination.”

Lurlene. Lurlene’s locker. “How much is the pawn ticket for?”

"Five hundred dollars."

The amount of her insurance deductible. Her jewelry was worth far more. "Could I pay the pawn ticket?"

"It's not that simple. Do you have any pictures of the jewelry, any way to identify it?"

She had, of course, the photos required by her insurance company. Wordlessly she rummaged in her desk, handing him an envelope.

He examined its contents, looking relieved. "This should do it." He stood, holding the pictures. "I really thank you." He turned to leave.

She felt kicked, empty. "What happens next?"

"I'll send the police up later so you can file charges. You realize that while The Oaks regrets this happened, you hired this individual privately. Although she is on our staff and can be dismissed for any felony, we did not recommend her to you for private employment." He was getting The Oaks off the hook.

A felony charge. Future jobs jeopardized. Questions by any training program...Mitylene. "What if I don't file charges?"

"But we need this. Don't you want the girl punished?"

"I don't know."

His annoyance was obvious. "Look, Clare, I have to get back to Security. We'll talk later." He left, the pictures grasped tightly.

Alone she felt her pulse pounding. "It's my own fault," she kept thinking. "I knew. I should have done something not to let it happen." A wave of nausea engulfed her. She dreaded seeing the girl, hated herself because she did not know what to do.

By 3:20 Lurlene had not come. On her walker Clare took the elevator down to the basement. Past the row of employee lockers she could see Lurlene hunched on a bench, sucking on an almost empty Pepsi bottle.

Clare confronted her. "I trusted you." She stared, watching the girl's face crumble.

"I didn't steal nothing. Just borrowed them things. I was going to get them back, put them back."

"I cared about those things. They belonged to my mother."

Lurlene's dark eyes flashed resentfully. "You don't care about your Mama. Why you care about her stuff?"

Clare flinched.

Lurlene's voice became wheedling. "You ain't going to be calling no policeman…'

Clare's gaze remained steady, unwavering. "I cared about you."

The voice rose to a high-pitched wail. "No. No you don't. Don't nobody care about me." Lurlene snuffled. "Not Mitylene, not my auntie, not Clarence."

For a moment Clare wanted to take the child into her arms, to tell her everything would be all right. Until she saw the look of pure hatred. Drawing back, she clamped her lips together and said nothing.

"You one mean white woman. Just like your Mama."

Silently Clare turned. Braced by her walker, shoulder muscles twinging, she made her way back to the elevator, toward her empty apartment.

Tomorrow she would drive herself to the bookstore. Reenroll in her old book club. Determinedly she took a deep breath. Then to Wal-Mart for a cell phone, the kind with the prepaid minutes because they were cheaper. And finally she would buy a deck of cards for the games with Julia and Mary Alys.

RAPTOR 1976

She had, he realized too late, robbed him of his manhood. Deft as a female spider, she had ensnared him in tendrils of ease and convenience.

He lay flat on his back, hands folded behind his head as he stared ceilingward in the morning half-light. Beside him the low hum of her snoring. Her flesh which had once seemed soft and inviting, now he perceived as flabby, portending an early descent into shapeless fat.

He had been young and directionless then, a senior in college, whose mother exulted in his IQ, a father who pressured him. She had seemed an oasis: the daughter of a Marine killed in Iraq, and a mother now re-married and living in Idaho, she appeared before him untrammeled by filial obligations.

Lost in the comfort and convenience of her bed, he had slid unquestioning into the ease of assignments researched and typed for him, roast chicken simmering whenever he appeared.

Unlike him, she had known what she wanted. And what she had wanted was him. Him married to her. Him in med school. And now, six years later, him in this one-bedroom apartment five blocks from University Hospital where, in this first year of residency, his life now centered.

She had become peripheral to him. A shadow rising each morning to pack her lunch, cross the street to the bus stop from which she left for whatever government building where she programmed computers, or something. Dutifully, without joy or pride, he took her on Friday nights to the keg parties of his fellow residents and med students. There she sat in a corner, smiling but not understanding the in-jokes, stifling a yawn. Scarcely alive to him.

What was alive was Ginger. Ginger, whose blond hair hung haphazardly down over her white jacket, who straggled to keep up with the gaggle of med students behind the attending. Helpless, hopeless and adorable, the only girl in this small rotation of third year students. She would have never been accepted for med school were it not for her father, a Department head with political clout, a mother on every Board in town. Money.

Money. It showed in the imperious tilt of Ginger's head, the light laughter when she flubbed a question from the attending, whom she had known since childhood as "Uncle Joe".

He should have resented her. Instead his heart leapt up when she commandeered him to drive her home. The careless half-glance upward at him from dark-fringed violet eyes. "What would I ever do without you?'

In the soul numbing grind of no sleep and scut work, her obvious need for him wakened him to life. His blood began to circulate again, pooling in that area unmentionable in staid society.

"But you're married," she had laughed. She had pulled her arm from his guiding hand, turning away with what he recognized as a come-hither look as she slid from the cubicle in which trainees on call tried to snatch interrupted sleep.

"And if I weren't?"

"But you are." She smiled, and was gone from him.

He thought of divorce. But thought of the struggles necessary to escape his uxorious burden exhausted him. His parents, who had first warned of an unripe marriage, now luxuriated in the unseen web she had diligently spun around them. They expected their son to be grateful because she had gotten him "back on track", her salary paying the young couple's living costs, while they antied up his tuition.

Instead the demanded gratitude rose like bile in his resentment-constricted throat.

Six months ago she had placed before him, (a copy emailed to his businessman father), concise data on the advantages of buying a house now. So that in two years, when she became pregnant…

He felt as if breath were sucked from his lungs, as if he were being pulled into an awaiting abyss.

She managed everything; he, a hapless victim to her unrelenting care, as she anticipated his every need before he might feel it himself. Lying in an insomniac's darkness beside her, his fingers clinched and unclenched as he contemplated the release her demise might provide him. Unfortunately he would be caught, jailed at the mercy of gorilla-shouldered perverts. Still rational although defeated, he relinquished his solacing dream of mayhem

Until The Lecture. By a visiting VIP from Hopkins, who warned of the diagnostic perils of those medications whose potential morbidity left no trace.

Hope surged again within him. His freedom could be free! Not now, he soothed himself, but SOON.

It was the routine Friday pm beer bust. Ginger, in a shimmering silk sheath, arrived on the arm of a wooden-faced. dark-suited stranger, as alien among the blue-jeaned beer swillers as his own unwanted matrimonial baggage.

The beat of an African rhythms throbbed beneath a sinuous trumpet solo, surging upward. In a moment of passion and compassion, he rescued Ginger and flung her out into tiny space cleared by a circle of their chanting colleagues. Watched her shimmy before him, the electricity between them palpable. His hips gyrating in a euphoria he had never before known, he heard the chant rise to a high pitch of expectation.

Until the dark-suited arm, immaculate white cuff extending a proper half inch, grabbed the swirling Ginger from him. A low stern-voiced command: “We’re leaving.”

Empty-armed, drenched in perspiration and limp from exertion, he turned his gaze upon his wife, anticipating her jealous pout. She glanced at her Timex.

The next morning, bleary-eyed, he dragged himself to the Saturday rounds required of all trainees by “Uncle Joe”. Instead of the sullen white-coated entourage, trailing like *fluor albus* behind their leader, a larger huddle ringed the tall figure of the attending, who was actually smiling.

Unable to see into the circle’s center, he elbowed himself into its outer fringe and demanded of a fellow resident “What…?”

“Ginger just rescued the old man from death by dilemma“

Still trying to eye the elusive center of the group, “Huh? How’d she do what?”

“Got herself engaged. The guy’s whisking her off to Hong Kong. No more med school. So old Joe won‘t be caught between her enraged Papa if he fails her, or a malpractice suit when she kills somebody.”

At that moment the head nurse turned aside and Ginger, from inside the sparkling bubble of her presence, raised her left hand to wave, ring finger extended. A two caret rock glittered under the hissing florescent tube overhead. And then she turned her back.

She was lost to him, lost before he could free himself for her. Laughing and leaving. He felt like a shriveled balloon from which all air had escaped.

In the early dusk, he arrived back at the apartment, hungry and in need of solace. No amber lamplight glowed in the darkened window. Inside, silence. He flicked the light switch and made his way toward the recliner, confused. Where was his dinner, his wife handing him an open beer?

He felt a mild annoyance. He did not know where she was. Not that he cared where she was, but the inconvenience of not knowing intruded into his routine.

He wandered to the fridge; in the cool gust, he beheld a white saran-topped casserole dish: “Microwave - three minutes”.

Fretfully he closed the fridge door. Maybe in the bedroom? Past the neatly made bed, he saw the open doors of their closet: well-ironed shirts immaculately hung on blue plastic hangars. His slacks and sports jackets seemed to have more space between them, no longer crowded by blouses, her blue raincoat.

Confused, he returned to the recliner and sank into its welcoming depths. Automatically his hand sought the remote on the end table beside it. His fingers brushed a square envelope. He flicked on the TV, before opening the unsealed missive.

Against the glare of the TV screen, his eyes squinted at her precise, upright script.

"I am writing because I do not know how to tell you this in person.

"I have met someone else. I know it is wrong, but it just happened. I will be living with two girls from the office while I file for divorce.

"I hope you will not contest. George is well prepared and able to foot the bills for any legal struggles that ensue

.

"I am truly sorry. I hope you meet someone who will love you as you deserve.

"Give my regards to your wonderful parents. They are so proud of you."

At first he thought this was some ploy, some machination to evoke a reaction from him, send him scurrying to fetch her. He turned the envelope over. There was no return address. He saw his hand crumple the paper into a wad and hurl it across the room.

She was gone. His breath came in short, shallow gasps. It was not that her departure mattered. What irritated him was the feeling that something had been done to him against his will, a possession stolen. What would people think?

His father....his father would be angry. He hoisted himself from the recliner, and from the top shelf of a kitchen cabinet pulled down the bottle of Scotch she kept for his father's visits. He poured the brown liquid into a coffee mug, and trudged back to his recliner.

As he swigged down half the mug's contents, he became cognizant of the injustice of a wife deserting her husband midway through his crucial first year of residency. By the time he had emptied the mug, his head was clear and a major truth was revealed to him which would sustain him through three marriages to come. He, hardworking and innocent soul that he was, had been taken advantage of. His wife was a Bitch.

WIDE WORLD WAITING

Saturday, Columbus Day Weekend, 2007

Maddie sat in the front pew of the small chapel, trying to smile despite the dread that fluttered at the base of her throat. With her left hand, she stroked the worn walnut bench beneath her, wood sawn and sanded by her father's hands almost seventy years ago.

She sucked in a breath of autumn air from the open casement windows. The air was scented with pine boughs she had last night placed under each window to freshen the musty chapel.

Beside her Delia, second cousin and companion of her childhood. Delia, who would not let her sit alone at this wedding of her grandson. Behind them sat a small gathering of relatives. Now, after half a century away, she had returned a stranger among them, feeling no warmth of kinship. Only with her grandson, Alden.

More important were those not here: Her daughter Christi, whose voice on the phone had been ragged, “Mother, can't you stop him? Tell him at twenty-three he should have sense enough not to take on trailer trash with two kids.”

But she could not stop this marriage any more than she could stop Christi, six hundred miles away in Houston, from going with her husband to the Homecoming Game. Choosing to see their younger daughter in the Beauty Walk rather than attending their son's wedding.

Maddie bit her lip; she felt Delia's reassuring touch on her arm. For a moment she wished Lois had driven up from the Gulf coast. Lois knew what it was like to be an Air Force wife, living all over the world, their lives scattered among communities which dissolved behind them. Until she and Hal had returned, as they always knew they would, to this family land where she was born.

She listened to the hesitant strains of wedding hymns, coaxed from the old pump organ by the bride's thin-haired younger brother. The music was soft and restrained, as if the thin-haired young man sensed exuberance would not be appropriate.

Determinedly Maddie raised her chin, forced a smile onto her lips, trying to dredge up hope: for Alden, for all of them.

The organ segued into a muted processional. At the side entrance she glimpsed Alden, rawboned and awkward in his National Guard uniform, black bow tie slightly askew. With a pang, she realized he did not own a dark suit. Her hand moved up, as if to straighten his tie.

Beside Alden stood the Reverend Cheatham, a retired minister who had driven the twenty-seven miles from Ridgemont. Two years ago he had made this same trip to bury her mother, then last November, Hal.

She heard the murmur from the congregation behind her and turned to see six- year-old Mark march down the aisle, half dragging his little sister, Emily, who forgot to strew rose petals from the basket she gripped. A wave of tenderness engulfed Maddie. Certainly any mother who could produce such children couldn't be all bad. She watched Alden reach out and place his hand on the boy's shoulder.

And then a collective gasp from those watching: Kathy, her pale pink strapless gown shimmering in a shaft of late afternoon sunlight; Kathy, slender, blond, head high in the proud awareness of her own beauty.

Alden's eyes were on Kathy as she approached the pulpit; his hand still on Mark's shoulder. The four of them faced the minister, their backs to the congregation. .Kathy's blond ringlets cascaded down from a short pink veil over her tanned shoulders.

"Dearly beloved, we are gathered here today to unite in holy matrimony a new family."

Whispers among those behind her at this deviation from familiar rites.

The minister did not stand behind the pulpit. Instead he bent down before the children, intoning familiar but now altered words: "Mark, do you take Alden for your father, from this day forward to love, honor and obey him?"

The earnest young voice, "Yes, sir."

"And do you, Emily, take Alden to be your Dad, and promise to love and obey him?"

A pause. Then Mark's firm response. "She does."

Maddie blinked her eyes to hold back tears, as she watched the minister carefully turn the children to face the congregation.

"Mark, take Emily over to sit with Mr. and Mrs. Grover so you can watch the rest of the ceremony." Elmer Grover,

Alden's boss at the Ridgemont Motor Pool; his wife, Stella, who ran the tanning salon where Kathy worked.

Emily, seeing Maddie, almost bolted toward her but Mark's grasp on her wrist was tight.

If only, Maddie wished, Kathy had arranged for Emily to sit with her.

Later, at the reception in the old school house next door, Maddie breathed easier, relieved that the yellow roses from her garden had not wilted, that the redheaded teenager she had hired was replenishing chicken salad sandwiches, pouring fresh pineapple sherbet into the punch bowl.

It was over. The bride, now changed into a blue velour pantsuit, handed her bouquet to Mark and whispered something into his ear. Then aloud: "Y'all mind, Maddie and Stella." The three-day week-end with Maddie, then to Stella's because it was near Mark's school in Ridgemont, near Emily's baby-sitter.

And they were gone. Into Alden's red truck for a honeymoon at the Gulf Coast where, two years earlier, hurricane Katrina had ravaged their lives.

Under the sun's slanting rays, Maddie watched Mark stride across the cemetery, white bridal bouquet in hand, and place it on Hal's grave. Taking Emily's hand into hers, she turned toward the reception hall and the clean-up tasks awaiting her.

June 1998

He had first come to them the summer he was fourteen, gangly, with the hang-dog look of a kid who knew he did not please his father. He was a middle child, bracketed on each side by beautiful blond sisters.

Her daughter Christi had called from Houston with a pressured plea. This summer she would be driving the girls to Junior Miss pageants; her husband had business trips. What to do with Alden was a problem.

Maddie and Hal were living on the Gulf coast then, Hal retired from the military and earning three times as much as a civilian, Maddie working for the local welfare office. "It's a chance to get to know our grandson." she had told Hal. They cancelled a trip to Alaska where they had planned to visit their son David and his wife at their marine biology station.

Alden did not talk much, but she noticed that he made his bed each morning, carried his dinner dishes to the sink. She watched him gradually relax from hang dog to following in Hal's footsteps like a young puppy.

He came back to them each summer, riding the bus, clothes in a duffle bag. She saw his taut mien relax as Hal, in the easy-going manner with which he dealt with young mechanics under his tutelage, taught him to run their small boat, to repair motors.

On weekends, as she drove up to Randolph Crossing to tend her elderly parents, she was glad Alden was with Hal. They were both glad when he enrolled in a junior college on the Mississippi Coast. By then her father had died and she and Hal had moved back to West Alabama. Alden came up weekends to help Hal build their large addition onto her mother's small house. She had seen the careful attention on Alden's face as Hal pointed out how their large new den would open onto a small hall by her mother's bedroom. She had watched, smiling, as Hal and Alden hauled large stones for the fireplace.

She remembered how proud and happy the two of them had been, and for this memory she was grateful

February 2004

She had cooked his favorite dinner that weekend. "I've signed up for the National Guard down at school," Alden mentioned between mouthfuls of black-eyed peas and sweet potato casserole, "to help pay for college."

She despaired. He had not asked their advice, had not considered the possible consequences. Before Katrina hit, his unit was already deployed to Iraq. Maddie was terrified that he would not survive because there was something unformed about him, unperceiving of possible perils.

"He'll make it," Hal tried to reassure her. "I did." But Hal had never been faced with killing others to survive. A mechanic whom pilots depended upon for safe planes, his mission had been to protect lives, not to destroy them.

In early summer her mother died, slipping silently from life in her sleep. Maddie, numb, could feel no comfort in the condolence of cousins. Only in tending her mother's garden, with the soil between her fingers - earth her mother had nurtured - did she find solace. On her knees in the garden, transplanting fragile roots, she felt a connection with the land humming in every cell of her body. At peace in a landscape that felt right to her.

Miraculously Alden survived. He came back to a college collapsed by Katrina, then to his parents in Texas, and finally, confused and lost, back to them.

Hal found him a job in the Motor Pool in Ridgemont, from which he returned each weekend, reaching for the too-heavy loads Hal tried to hoist, steadying the ladder on which Hal faltered, and finally standing beside her in the November rain of Hal's funeral. It was Alden who stayed, while Christi and her family left for a football game in Tuscaloosa before flying home to Houston. Alden stayed after her son David flew down from Alaska, tested the well water, bought her a new computer and installed a rooftop antenna before returning to his wife and their work. Each weekend Alden drove Hal's red pickup home from Ridgemont, brought in her firewood and avoided Hal's empty recliner by the fireplace.

May 2007

She should have known, when he first asked, between mouthfuls of turnip greens and cornbread, "Do they still have that picnic down at the cemetery?"

"You mean Decoration Day?" She thought of the young plants she had ready for Hal's grave.

"I was wondering," he swallowed hesitantly. "There's this woman....with two kids. They've moved to Ridgemont so she can work in Stella's tanning place. They don't know anybody."

"Of course you can bring them," she answered his unspoken request, pleased with his concern for strangers, thinking that she would bring a baked ham, potato salad to provide for the extra mouths.

"I can haul a case of cokes over." He was maturing, she noted; he was taking responsibility.

Decoration Day 2007

She had not seen them when they arrived. On her knees, transplanting zinnias and marigolds, her view was blocked by a gardenia bush. When she struggled to her feet, she glimpsed Alden, standing under the backboard, tossing a basketball to a slender, brown-haired child. She gazed across the clearing, among the groups of familiar faces, but did not see a woman who might be the boy's mother.

She hurried into the old school building to wash the dirt from her hands.

Inside the doorway, Delia was arranging fried pies on a large platter.

"Have you seen the woman Alden…?"

"Everybody's seen her," Delia interrupted, "Alden's got himself a real looker."

"Where…?"

Delia's gaze followed her beer bellied husband, Ernie, who shoved his way into a cluster of young males under an oak tree. "No fool like an old fool," she muttered.

Sitting on a bench in the group's center was a slender blond girl in dark glasses, wearing a rose colored sun-dress. At her side a small girl struggled with a chain of clover blossoms.

"But she's so young," Maddie gasped.

"Old enough," snorted Delia as she tugged the rope of the school bell, announcing dinner.

Maddie made her way past neighbors lining up before the buffet tables, toward the clearing where the girl and child remained seated. The girl was a stranger here, uncertain, with two children. Maddie felt a rush of warmth, of sympathy. She felt a wisp of hope for the understanding which might rise between them as she reached out her hand in welcome.

She saw the girl's eyes shift away from her, toward the field from which Alden approached, basketball in hand, the boy at his side.

"This," he said to his grandmother who stood waiting beside the girl, "is Kathy."

She should have known that evening, when she watched Alden put his jacket around the girl's bare shoulders. Should have known when he asked to bring her to Maddie's that next weekend. "She needs to get the kids out of that hot trailer."

Somewhere deep within her, she had realized that if she did not allow this, despite the warning chill within her, she might lose him. She needed him. Not just for the help he offered, but needed to see him, to feed him, to know that he was all right. "It's your home," she said in a compromise that age had taught her.

Later, when he queried "Gran, isn't Kathy a wonderful girl?" she had hedged uncomfortably, "I really don't know her."

Maddie tried. In the early dusk she approached Kathy, who sat on the swing watching Alden repair a broken gate. Across the lawn Mark and Emily chased lightening bugs.

When she approached, Kathy did not shift her position in welcome.

Maddie sank down onto the swing beside her. "Your children are certainly well-behaved."

Kathy eyed her warily. "I've had to keep them on a tight leash. You don't know what it's like, trying to raise kids by yourself, among strangers, with nobody around to depend on."

But Maddie did know, suddenly remembering.

November 1962

She, Hal and their two children had been in Spain only four weeks, transferred from Germany. Away from the 97th General hospital, where Christi had been born three years earlier, David the past year. Away from the sisterhood of young military wives, the base housing with its commissary and PX.

They were temporarily billeted in a Spanish hotel from which each morning Hal drove their old Opal forty-eight kilometers to an Air Base under construction. The only American family at the hotel, she knew no one and could speak only a few words of Spanish. And then the call: Hal on alert because of the Cuban missile crisis, stuck in a cork-padded room to oversee in-air-re fueling of American bombers which circled the sky but never landed.

From her window Maddie stared down at Franco's green-uniformed Civil Guards, always in pairs, rifles slung across their shoulders. Terrified at how they might react to anyone from the U. S. she waited for two days in their cramped quarters. On the third day she ran out of milk, of bread, of eggs.

She knew she had to do this. She strapped David into his stroller, grasped Christi's hand so tightly the child yelped, and set out. Fear clutched her insides lest they become separated, lest she lose them in this strange land where every tree must be watered to survive. She pushed the stroller, half dragged Christi along the stone pathway between narrow buildings, up a slope, not knowing what lay over the hill.

Finally she had come upon a bakery with flat loaves hanging in the window. She handed the woman a twenty-peso note, and was beset by the reality that beyond a few Spanish banknotes, she had only Army script.

Back in their quarters her hand shook as she spooned cereal into David's mouth, wiped his chin. Beside her, Christi was crying, an ongoing desolate wail that echoed her own despair. She was unable to reach for Christi, to comfort her.

"I can't do this anymore," she had thought. "I have to, but I can't." It was the first time she could no longer command herself to do what was required.

Every cell in her body longed to go home, to forsake this foreign world for the familiar red-rutted roads of West Alabama. To hand the children over to her mother, to sit on the porch and await her father's nightly homecoming from his sawmill job .To watch him use the last daylight tending his crops.

Her insides ached with a terrible homesickness. But there was no way she could return, no way she could afford plane tickets for herself and the children, or even third class fares on a ship.

If only she could hear her parents' voices. But an overseas call cost money she and Hal did not have.

She could send a telegram to her father, ask for the money. He would sell his truck, borrow against their land, send the money he had saved for taxes, somehow bring them home. And then what? Would Hal desert his post to follow, risk court martial?

This could not be. Resolutely she took Christi onto her lap.

She stayed. Within the week, Hal was back with them, dead-tired, sleeping. Gradually her world righted itself. In the years afterward she wondered what might have happened if, just once, she had made a wrong choice.

Spring 1964

They were back Stateside: Hal on temporary duty in Delaware for two months; Maddie and the children home with her parents in Randolph Crossing.

Back from the arid Spanish landscape into an Alabama spring: white pear blossoms against a blue sky; air fragrant with wild honey suckle. Her mother was unable to move her happy gaze from the grandchildren she now saw for the first time. Her father's quiet pride, relatives with outstretched arms, laps ready for her children to climb onto. Mornings when she awoke she gazed through the window of her childhood bedroom at sunlight glinting on shiny leaves of an elm tree. A world both known and right.

Her mother had taken David down to the pasture to watch tadpoles in the shallows of a brook. Christi was off for the morning with Hal's aunt. Maddie felt a sudden, unfamiliar lightness; burdens she did not realize she carried, now lifted. For the first time in years she was unfettered by demands of what needed to be done.

In the fresh morning air, she climbed the hill behind her parents' house, up a long familiar path beneath pine trees, past rhododendron and wild azaleas. Pausing on a rock-cropped ridge, she looked down on the roof of her parent's home, her mother's vegetable garden with its neat borders of fresh young greens.

She had never before realized how small her parent's house was. In the damp winters of Germany, she had washed her children's clothes at the base laundromat, and longed for the sun-dried smell of sheets from her mother's clothes line. She had taken for granted her mother's unceasing toil: canning tomatoes and okra over a wood-stove in August, darning socks by a bare overhead light bulb in winter, sweeping the kitchen with its oil-cloth-covered table. "Folks feel better in an orderly house," her mother had murmured. Until now she had not realized how little her parents had, how much they had given her.

Always she had gone to school in a freshly ironed blouse, her lunch pail contained an extra boiled egg, a roasted sweet potato, or peach for the teacher to place in lunch for “a poor child”.

Below her, to the left, she saw the collapsed roof of the shack where those red-headed poor children had lived in an unpainted cabin with dirt floors. Beside its vine-covered crumbling ruins a trailer now stood. But the yard was still cluttered with a broken sawhorse, old tires.

She rose and followed the path up the hill. Like an epiphany, it struck her: she knew what was on the other side of the hill, was certain of her way back home. Her muscles were no longer taut with apprehension. She inhaled deeply with the wonder of how much easier her life here was.

She remembered leaving home that first time. As Hal loaded their suitcases into his old Dodge, she had clung to her mother with a premonition of long separations to come.

Her mother’s mouth against her ear, the whispered solace. “There’s a wide world waiting for you, honey.” From a mother who had never ventured farther from her birthplace than the scant hundred miles to Montgomery. Dredging up from unknown depths those words which had sustained her daughter for so long.

In the afternoon she had visited Delia. Two high school friends had come over.

“Where’ve you been these five years?” asked Betty Sue who, like Delia, had put on weight since high school.

“Germany. Spain…” For so long she had looked forward to telling them about her life there, about Franco’s grip.

"I got a cousin in France," interrupted Nancy Jean. "Used to play football for Leesville. They got a good football team in Spain?"

Maddie cleared her throat to explain about soccer.

Nancy Jean interrupted. "Delia, you hear about Ike Tubeville and that cheerleader?"

Maddie had sat there, smiling politely, feigning interest but feeling isolated. It wasn't their fault, she told herself, they didn't listen to the nightly news for a clue as to where Hal might be shipped next. Theirs was simply a different world. But she could never again shake that lonely feeling, the recognition that she had become an outsider among them.

At the end of two months, when Hal had come to load her and children into the second-hand station wagon she was ready to go, again eager to see what lay over the next hill.

Summer 2007

Every weekend Alden brought Kathy and the children to her. From her kitchen window Maddie watched the kids scamper from the red Ford truck into the yard. Watched Alden haul luggage and supplies into her mother's part of the house, Kathy following with a small tote bag.

"You doing okay, Gran?" Alden asked, coming into her kitchen, raising the lid from a pot on the stove. "Sure smells good."

"Where's Kathy?"

"Changing clothes before supper. Guess I ought to get cleaned up myself", and out he wandered.

He was, she noted, happier, more centered. For this, she knew she had Kathy to thank. Yet she could not submerge her feeling of antipathy for the girl, a gut feeling.

The girl was not impolite, only elusive, her bland smile somehow not extending upward into her eyes. Maddie sighed, frustrated with herself, because in truth she spent her lonely weekdays looking forward to their arrival, planning what she would cook, ordering books for the children. She could not bring herself to think what her life would be like without these weekends. She had no right to her misgivings but they persisted.

On Sunday morning, as Alden lugged two laundry bags of clothes to the washer and dryer in her kitchen she asked "Shouldn't Kathy be doing this?" She tried to conceal the edge to her voice.

"She's tired, Gran. Taking care of the kids, working at the tanning place. I worry about her."

But Maddie could not help noticing: the girl did not get up Sunday mornings to supervise her children, sent them evenings to watch TV. She saw, with apprehension, the sudden glimmer of interest on Kathy's face as she stared at a photograph on the wall.

"These your folks, Alden?" The picture was of Christi, her husband, and their three teenagers, before their impressive brick Tudor.

Alden seemed unconcerned. "Yeah, in Houston. Back when I was in high school."

Maddie could not read the girl. She wished Hal were here, wished she could discuss her impressions with him. They had balanced each other; without him, she was less certain of herself. She wrote an e-mail to Lois, trying to explain her bad vibes about Kathy, but then, ashamed, deleted it.

So she was relieved when Alden, on a Wednesday evening, drove over from Ridgemont without Kathy.

"I need to talk with you, Gran. About Kathy." He pushed back the remains of peach cobbler she had fixed for dessert.

He's beginning to see the difficulties, she thought hopefully. She watched him twist his hands together and struggle for words.

"She's had a rough time."

She listened, at first hoping that somehow he might explain the girl to her, help her understand what lay behind Kathy's haughty aloofness.

At first she resonated with sympathy as she heard that Kathy's alcoholic parents had been killed in a wreck when Kathy was fifteen. Sorrowed at the thought of her being sent to a strict grandmother in Hattiesburg whom she hated. At seventeen when Kathy became pregnant with Mark, her young husband had taken her home to live with his mother. But the mother-in-law was even stricter than her grandmother.

Now, in the hot August night as the air conditioning cycled on and off, Maddie watched her grandson struggle with depths of feeling new to him. He would have given up foundering for words were it not for her persistent questions. She saw his anguish at what he perceived as the undeserved misfortunes of Kathy's life but which Maddie recognized as something else. Despair gnawed at her stomach as she pieced together Kathy's history.

On her nineteenth birthday, stir- crazy, Kathy had left Mark with her despised mother-in-law and caught a bus to

Biloxi. She was young, lost. A dealer at the casino offered to "take care of her." By the time her young husband finally arrived with Mark, she chose to stay with the older man. The next year she let herself become pregnant by him, hoping he would divorce his wife and marry her. When he did not, she wanted desperately to leave but with two small children where could she go? She waited, miserable.

Until the evacuation warnings for Katrina. In the pelting rain, Emily's father had stood outside the screen door, shoving inside to her a damp envelope full of cash. He was leaving, driving his wife and sons to Oklahoma. He told her to take Mark and Emily inland to Hattiesburg where her grandmother and Mark's father could help.

Instead, relieved to be finally free, she drove with a girl friend to Birmingham. The children cried, the girl friend left. An overeager Rehab counselor found housing, money and a stipend for an LPN program Kathy did not want to attend. Alone, with two children, she saw no other choice.

She had already given up on classes when she ran into Stella, whom she remembered from high school. Again desperate, with no place to go, she had come to Ridgemont to work in Stella's tanning salon. But the trailer Stella's husband found for her was in a drug-infested area.

It was almost midnight and Maddie was bone weary as she heard Alden's anguished plea. "She just needs a chance, Gran..."

Maddie gripped the arms of her chair. Alden was too naïve, did not perceive the slippery slope of despair along which Kathy might drag him. She was too tired to mince words. "It sounds like she's had a great many chances and hasn't made very wise decisions."

She saw the steeling of his jaw, the shadow of anger across his face. “She needs me, Gran. The kids need me.” He paused. “I’m going to marry her.”

It was as if a mule had kicked Maddie in the stomach. “What if she gets pregnant, can’t work?” Surely he would recognize that on his salary he couldn’t take this on.

“She won’t get pregnant…”

Maddie waited, her silence demanding an answer.

And then from the terrible depths of him: “She was all by herself in Birmingham. She had an abortion. They tied her tubes.”

She saw what the admission cost him. He was taking this burden onto himself, foreclosing the possibility of children of his own. Obviously exhausted, he rose and headed toward his bedroom. “I had thought,” he muttered wearily, “maybe we could be a family.”

September 2007

“Kathy’s never had a real wedding, Gran. She wants to get married down here, in the chapel.”

Maddie tried to sound the girl out on her plans.”If you have the ceremony here, Alden’s relatives will expect to be invited.”

Kathy smiled her non-committal smile and shrugged.

Maddie persisted. “Are you planning a reception?”

“Alden says that whatever you arrange will be nice. Since they’re your kin, you know what they want”. Again, she smiled at Maddie dismissively.

Why, Maddie wondered, can she make me feel guilty, like I'm trying to take over, when she's refusing to do anything herself? She recalled a phrase at the welfare office: the gimme-gimme-gimme phooey syndrome.

The next week Kathy unexpectedly came into her living room while Alden was up in the pasture. "Alden says we'll be living here after the wedding. I want to talk to you."

Finally, Maddie thought, she's going to thank me for offering this, ask what she can do to help in exchange for living here rent free.

Kathy slid into the usually empty recliner by the fireplace. "I've been accepted in an LPN course at Ridgemont Hospital."

Confused, Maddie did not respond.

"Aren't you going to congratulate me?"

Maddie tried to compute in her head the loss of Kathy's salary, the cost of day care for Emily. "Can you afford it?"

"We can't afford for me not to. So long as I'm enrolled in classes, Alden won't have pay on my student loans in Birmingham."

Bile rising in her mouth, Addie did not reply.

"I'm really doing this for Alden and the children."

Maddie wondered what the girl was getting at.

"But I won't be able to study if I have to worry about the children."

Maddie waited.

"I'm going to let Emily stay with you days. But I have to know that you'll take good care of her, or I'll worry. And that you'll be here when Mark gets off the school bus afternoons." Again the smile that was supposed to be charming but wasn't. "Emily doesn't mind staying with you."

Mind, thought Maddie angrily. Emily loves me. Maddie clenched her teeth together. It's for Emily, she told herself while she restrained herself from protesting, for Emily and for Alden. But in her heart she knew: it was for herself, because she feared that otherwise she would lose them all.

Sunday after the wedding

All day Maddie waited for their call, waited to summon the children to the phone to hear their mother's voice reassuring them. No call came.

In the morning she had bent down in the grass beside Emily to hold the tame guinea, as the child gently petted it. At lunch she watched Emily's face, waiting for her to cry when Emily realized her mother was not there. Neither child showed any distress as they munched cheese sandwiches, gulped down chocolate milk, and licked crumbs of their oatmeal cookies from their fingers.

While Emily napped, Maddie began an e-mail to Lois with details of the wedding. But Mark hung over her shoulder, asking questions, wanting to try the computer. She relented. Such an alert, curious child. It delighted her.

On Monday afternoon Maddie took the children's clothes from the dryer. Still no call from Alden and Kathy. Regretfully she packed Mark and Emily's few belongings in the brown paper sacks in which Kathy had sent them.

"Why can't we stay here?" Mark demanded.

I wish, she thought, but she did not want to stir Kathy's resentment by changing the girl's plans, challenging her authority. "Your mother wants you to be nearer your school. It's only until the weekend," she soothed. "Then you'll all be back here at home together."

She saw Mark dilly-dally at their departure, saw Emily's look of confusion in Ridgemont as Stella led her away from Maddie's car.

Wearily she returned to the silence of her own too-large house. On Tuesday she cleaned the rooms the children had left, went to the garden to pick the last of the tomatoes, the small, purple eggplant.

At dusk she sat by the phone, too tired to turn on the lights. She answered on the first sharp ring, "Alden?"

"Hi, it's me." Lois voice was strained. Lois who always e-mailed, rarely called. "Did you survive the nuptials?"

"I guess so."

"Are the children still there?"

"No. I'm alone," wondering what was underneath the pressure in Lois' voice.

"I need to talk with you….about Jennifer…"

Jennifer, Lois' only child, who must be in her mid-thirties by now, an Operating Room nurse at the med center in Birmingham. Perhaps Jennifer was marrying someone Lois disapproved of. Or maybe living with someone and not marrying.

"I'm driving up to visit her this weekend." Lois paused. "Are you up to an overnight guest?"

The sheets to be washed, the bathroom to be cleaned, the meals to cook. Her left shoulder ached from lifting Emily. She heard the desperation in Lois' tone. "It's fine," she said. "I look forward to seeing you."

Afterwards she sat in the recliner, remembering.

Colorado, 1971

She had known Lois since Jennifer was a baby. In Colorado, billeted next door to each other, their husbands both in 'Nam.

Maddie had longed to take Christi, then twelve, and David home to Randolph Crossing -- to be snug and secure during their anxious wait for Hal's return. But her practical side prevailed: she had base housing, the commissary. The children were in a good school. So she and Lois had waited out the year together, an unlikely pair who somehow clicked. Lois, a first-time mother in her late twenties, had left a coal mining town in Pennsylvania to work as a typist for the Air Force. In the Philippines she had met and married her radar-specialist husband, Michael.

Their husbands returned from Nam within a month of each other. But at their homecoming barbecue, Hal had seemed uncharacteristically ill-at-ease around the almost obscenely handsome Michael.

Within a month, Hal's orders for Texas came through. She and Lois stayed connected through Christmas cards those first few years, and then lost touch. Until more than twenty years later, at the Eglin PX on the Florida Gulf coast, she had glimpsed Lois, her brown hair now streaked blond, stunning in a black suit, a portfolio in hand. Over coffee, Lois happily told her of Michael's anticipated retirement. After thirty years of volunteering for far-flung posts where she and Jennifer could not follow, he would be home! In the meantime she was selling time-share condos quite successfully. It felt like yesterday when they had last seen each other. Amazed and delighted, they met regularly for lunch.

Until on a rainy night Lois, distraught, struggling against tears, was in their living room. Michael had come home only to announce he wanted out of the marriage. "I can do better," he muttered, leaving for San Francisco. Within a week, Lois had learned the full extent of the devastation he left behind: assets shifted to his name, bank account cleaned out, delinquent notices for Jennifer's nursing school tuition.

Maddie and Hall took her in, comforted her as best they could, and privately despaired that she could ever pull herself together. She did. She moved to Birmingham, frantically sold time-shares to Medical Center physicians, and managed to keep Jennifer in school. On trips to the coast, driving a van full of prospective buyers for courtesy weekends, she could scarcely squeeze in a coffee break with Maddie.

After Maddie's mother died, Lois, now back at the coast, loaned them her beachfront condo while she attended a real estate conference in Tallahassee. At Hal's death Lois offered to drive up, to bring Maddie down to the Gulf to recuperate. Numb, Maddie had been unable to leave the home Hal had built. Amid the sympathy of neighbors, of relatives, it was only Alden's presence that warmed her. During the week, when Alden was at work in Ridgemont, Lois' daily e-mails sustained her.

Now, on Wednesday night, she still had not heard from Alden and Kathy. She and Lois sat before the great stone fireplace, small flames warming the October chill. Sated on her favorite seafood gumbo which Lois had brought, they sipped sangrias from Lois' cooler. Lois, the only person who did not expect to be cooked for, but who fed her.

"About Jennifer?" Maddie asked.

She saw Lois struggle to maintain her composure. "Jennifer's leaving," her voice cracked, "giving up everything: the O. R. job she loves, her beautiful townhome. Moving to San Francisco to take care of Michael." And then, almost a whisper, from deep within. "I wish the bastard were dead."

Her intensity jolted Maddie. So many years since the divorce; she'd assumed Lois was long over it. "Michael's sick?"

"AIDS." Calmer now. Into the silence. "He's gay."

"I didn't know…"

"Neither did I. But there was always a shadow between us. I thought it might be other women; he was away so much." Lois fell silent, carefully placed her sangria goblet on the table and stared into the fire.

Maddie remembered Hal's unease around Michael. Gently she tried to suggest: "He can't help it, being gay I mean."

"Hetero or homo, I don't give a dam, people should behave responsibly in relationships."

"How did you find out?"

"Two years after he left, he sent Jennifer a plane ticket to visit him in San Francisco, a graduation present. I should have had sense enough not to let her go. When she arrived, she found him living with some young creep."

Maddie watched the muscles in Lois neck tighten.

"She hadn't been there two days before this sleazebag suggested she join them in bed for a three-way 'sexual celebration'. .Jennifer literally ran out of the house and phoned me from the airport. I wired funds for a ticket. Afterwards I tried to get her into therapy but she didn't want to talk about it. Insisted that since nothing really happened, she didn't need counseling. But ever since, whenever she goes out with a guy for more than a few dates, she breaks it off."

"You never told me."

"You were busy with your parents, with Alden, with your job. I was ashamed of being so stupid, not recognizing what was going on, why he was shipping out on assignments so far away."

"Why, after all that, is Jennifer going to take care of him? Can't his gay lover do that?"

"Which one? Over the years, they've all left. He told her he doesn't have anyone else..."

"Except his daughter."

"She says it's her last chance to know her father." Lois shook her head. "Says it's what she's always wanted."

Maddie thought of Christi, of the richly travelled childhood she had provided her daughter. And now Christi lived in a sturdy brick house cocooned on a cul-de-sac, amid in-laws who had lived for three generations in Texas. Christi, who gave her own daughters modeling lessons, bought them the ball gowns she had longed for, cheered at football games which Maddie disdained. "It seems they always want what we don't give them."

The next morning they hiked across the brook, along a well-worn uphill path. Red and yellow sycamore trees overhead, fall leaves crunching beneath their feet. Maddie breathed deeply, inhaling aromas of a landscape she loved.

At the ridge they paused, looking down over the countryside below.

"How many acres do you own?" Lois asked.

"A hundred and sixty here. Eighty more across the road.

Gazing downward. Maddie saw where, on the back of the barn, a section of shingles had blown off. Call the roofer, she thought automatically, or perhaps Alden will...

"It must cost a fortune to keep this place up."

Maddie flinched, because it did. Plumbers, electricians, locksmiths from Ridgemont; all the tasks that Hal had so easily managed. After a lifetime of frugality. "Alden helps me..."

"Ever thought of selling?"

"Never."

"Some rich Northerners would pay a fortune for a retreat like this. .Good tax write-off."

Stunned, Maddie did not respond. Slowly they descended the rocky path.

"What would happen if you go sick...really sick?"

Maddie struggled not to remember: Hal gasping for breath, her call to 911, holding his hand, praying. It had seemed a lifetime, the forty-five minutes before the medics arrived to tell her it was too late.

"I worry about your living out here alone."

"I won't be alone. Alden, Kathy, the children...."

"What if they don't come back from the coast? What if Kathy gets down to Biloxi and wants to stay?"

"They have to come back. His job's in Ridgemont, the children..."

In the afternoon Lois brought out pictures of the gated community where she lived. "Mine's a townhouse, but you could buy a garden home with room to plant things."

Irritation stirred in Maddie. How could Lois?

"There's a clubhouse overlooking the bay, lots of other military families. We could travel together, go to concerts."

The price of friends was that they tried to control you by their caring. "Alden..." she protested.

"Sell him the place...."

Maddie laughed. "He couldn't begin to afford it. They'll be lucky to make ends meet living here rent free." She was relieved when Lois let the matter drop.

On Friday morning they loaded up Lois' blue Prius. "Are you sure you don't want to come with me? There's a Chinese exhibit at the Art Museum. I could drive you back here after lunch and still get to Jennifer's by five."

"I didn't know you cared about Chinese Art."

"I don't. But I try." Her face beaten and pleading.

In a farewell hug, she felt Lois' shoulders, thin and fragile. Lois, who now might never have grandchildren. She thought of Emily's damp hair against her cheek as she carried her from bath to bed, of Alden's young family filling her future. Unlike Lois, forlorn in a hollow life. Gratitude for her own good fortune warmed her.

All afternoon, while the deliveryman installed a new refrigerator in her mother's kitchen, happiness hummed inside her. Tomorrow they would be home, would bring the children.

At noon Saturday, he called. "Gran" There was static on the line. "I'm here, in Ridgemont, loading up a U-Haul. Is it okay if we come for supper?"

She longed to hear where they had gone, if they had had a good trip.

"It might be sort of late. So much to pack here."

The sun was setting when she heard the crunch of wide wheels on the gravel driveway. Hurrying down the porch steps, she glimpsed Alden lift Emily from the truck's cab, then reach a hand up toward Mark. She saw Mark turn away, his back to Alden and slide under the steering wheel to the opposite side of the cab and jump down.

Maddie reached out to hug Alden.

"I'm too sweaty." He backed away. "I need a shower."

Behind him she could see Mark poking into the truck, emerging with the two wrinkled brown grocery bags. No Kathy. She was probably following in the red pick-up.

She felt Emily lean against her. Hefting the child up, she felt Emily melt into her. They were all exhausted. "You go ahead and shower. I'll feed the children."

In the breakfast area she sat Emily, limply compliant, on a chair and wiped her face and hand with a warm wash cloth. "Mark," she called toward the bedrooms of her mother's house, "Supper." She placed their favorite chicken fingers and warm cinnamon rolls onto plates, spooned applesauce into small bowls.

Mark strode past her, grim-faced and silent, toward the TV in the den, fiddling with the remote. Then he walked toward the table and reached for his plate.

"Don't you want to eat here at the table?" she cajoled. "So you can see out the window when your mother drives up."

He looked at her defiantly. "She's not coming."

"Not coming?"

"She's in Texas." Plate in hand, he headed back to the TV and turned up the volume.

Alden wandered into the room, wearing an old terry-cloth robe of Hal's. He headed toward the counter, poured a mug of coffee, loading it up with four cubes of sugar. He gripped the cup with both hands as he gulped it down and sank into a chair.

Mark marched to the table, grasped Emily's plate and headed back toward the TV. "C'mon. Power Rangers are on."

Clutching a muffin in her fist, Emily slid down from her chair and followed.

Alden spooned casserole onto his plate.

"Mark says Kathy's in Texas."

He swallowed mouthful of casserole. "With my sisters, looking for an apartment."

"You drove out to Texas?"

"Kathy wanted to meet my folks." He wolfed down half a chicken finger before coming up for air. "They loved her," he said, enthusiastic for the first time since his arrival. "She fit right in."

"She's in Houston?" Maddie repeated, unable to take it in.

"Like I said: in Houston with Mom and my sisters, renting an apartment."

Her insides knotted up. "You're moving to Texas?"

He nodded. "My Dad got me a job there. Pay's great. More than twice as much as here."

"Doing what?"

"On an oil rig. Fourteen days on, then two weeks off. Works out real good. I can take care of the kids those weeks while Kathy's in school."

She sat there numb, a vacuum sucking at her insides. "How long can you stay here?" Thinking of his job in Ridgemont, the notice he should give.

"Got to leave tomorrow. Early."

Maddie looked over at the children, Emily curled up on the floor, her head on a sofa pillow, eyes closed.

"I figure there won't be much traffic on the interstate on Sunday. We ought to get there by night."

"You're driving it in one day?"

"Got to. Unload the truck Monday, report to the company Tuesday morning."

Stunned, she tried to take the words in. They were leaving. "It's almost six hundred miles," she protested. "You're all exhausted. The children..."

"They don't have to do anything, just sit in the cab, sleep if they want." He finished eating, wiped his mouth, and took his plate to the sink. "Sure will miss your cooking, Gran." He hesitated. "I'll miss you, this place. But Kathy never was too keen about moving out here." He shook his head wearily. "This is the only way I can earn enough to give her what she deserves."

He stood by the sink, seeming to ponder. "You know, I never expected my Dad to do anything like this for me." He yawned. "I better turn in. I'm half dead. Hey, Mark, bring your plate and Emily's over here to the sink."

She felt like a balloon with the air escaping. She took a deep breath, pulled herself up from the table, and carried a sleepy Emily toward her bath.

Afterwards she knocked on Alden's door, heard him rouse himself, a mumbled "Come in".

She stood in the doorway. In the dim light from the hall she saw him prop himself up on an elbow amid a tangle of covers.

"Leave the children here. Just for the week. I'll drive Mark over to Ridgemont to school every day." She was pleading. "Next Saturday I'll drive them to Houston." She could not see his expression. "I'll get Lois to come with me. We'll take two days, have time for rest stops."

And his muttered response: "Kathy warned me."

"Warned you?"

"That you'd try to keep them. Get your friends at the Welfare Department to claim we're not fit parents, give you custody."

Appalled she heard the resentment rising from deep within him. She turned and left.

Alone in her own bed, she thought of calling Christi, of imploring her daughter not to be taken in by Kathy, not to be used. But it wouldn't work. She had long ago lost Christi. And now Alden.

When the phone rang, her first thought was Kathy, Kathy calling, finally, to talk with Mark and Emily. Answering, she felt her voice scratch in her throat.

"Maddie?" she heard Lois ask, "Am I waking you up?"

"No, I just finished putting Emily to bed. Where are you?"

"At Jennifer's. In her guest room."

"Oh?"

"Jennifer's leaving. There's nothing I can say, or do, that matters. She's going."

Maddie took a deep breath. "I'm sorry." From a lifetime's discipline she managed to pull up words which she hoped might help. "San Francisco's not the end of the world. You can fly out, visit her.
"

"And end up taking care of Michael, so Jennifer can have some life for herself? Lois' tone was bitter. "That's more than I can do." Lois fell silent. Then, almost a whisper, "I envy you: Alden, the children, a family."

Numbly Maddie forced herself to say the words: "They're going to Texas, Lois. Alden and the children are driving to Texas." Briefly she recounted the oil rig job.

"They're leaving you there by yourself?"

"I'll manage." She had never been really alone before. Always there had been people who cared: her parents, Hal, her children, Alden.

"You shouldn't be there alone." Lois, the manager, shifting into high gear. "I'm coming by there on my way back to the coast. I'm taking you back with me."

"I don't know."

"Just for a few days. Just to visit. Sit in the gazebo, look out over the bay. Relax and decide what you want to do. "

"I can't just leave…"

"Who was that neighbor Hal used to hire when you and he travelled?"

"Ezra. Ezra Lofton."

"I'll be there by four tomorrow afternoon, expecting you to have your bag packed." She heard the click of Lois hanging up.

In all her despair for a moment she had to laugh. Lois, the boss. Wearily she sank back onto her pillow.

Before dawn she arose, made biscuits filled with ham and scrambled eggs, peanut butter and jelly sandwiches, and placed them in a Styrofoam cooler along with bananas and apples. Chocolate milk for the children, Hal's old thermos full of strong coffee for Alden. She lugged it out to the U-Haul. A night wind chilled her to the bone. Emily would get cold. Back in her bedroom, she pulled the fleece throw from her bed, picked up a box of moist wipes, and took them back to the truck.

On the kitchen table she placed a hot casserole of cheese grits, the cinnamon buns re-warmed from last night. In the distance she heard a screen door clang shut.

As she dressed a drowsy Emily, she saw that Mark's bed was empty. Heard Alden's voice "Get in the truck, Mark."In the early morning half-light, she carried Emily down the porch steps.

The passenger door to the U-Haul stood open, Alden tightening a strap on Emily's car sear.

Maddie kissed the top of Emily's head, bent down to let Emily stand so that Alden could hoist her into the cab.

Suddenly she felt Emily clutching her, screaming. "No. Don't want to leave Nanna." Emily's grip tightened, her body shaking with sobs.

Her hand stroking Emily's hair, patting her shoulder, Maddie looked at her grandson, hoping.

Into the silence, from inside the truck, the flat voice of Mark. "You have to get in the truck, Emily. You have to let go and come get in the truck." She felt Emily's grip loosen.

Alden glanced at Maddie awkwardly, before he bent down and lifted the child into her car seat. "I guess this is goodbye" he muttered, buckling the strap. And then a low, "Thank you."

She wanted to say "Drive carefully", or "Call me when you get there, or "Promise to bring her back for a visit." She swallowed and said nothing.

She stood, watching him back the U-Haul out of the driveway onto the black top. Under the first rays of sunrise she watched them head into the wide world waiting.

Maddie shivered in the cold, looked down at the tender greens bordering the driveway. She bent down to pull out an invading weed, and slowly let a handful of loose soil filter through her outstretched fingers.

JUST DESSERTS

Hannah turned off the porch light and flipped the safety bolt on her front door. On the counter top beside the door a wicker basket of brownies, prepared for the parents of Halloween toddlers who might ring her doorbell. But none had come to this end apartment. Probably wise, she thought sadly, considering the hazards of poisoned candy.

She clicked off the overhead light and felt her way to the window, raising the blind. The parking space of the young couple next door was empty. Her own aged Corolla sat under the streetlight, its front bumper almost touching her walkway where yellow chrysanthemums bloomed.

Lonely she made her way toward the bedroom. She had invited her friend Jean over for supper and cider, but Jean had been afraid to leave her own home untended. "You never can tell what vandals might try." Hannah wondered what Jean, at eighty-six, could do. Call 911 on her cell phone, she supposed.

In her bedroom she closed the blinds, kicked off her shoes, and lay down on her bed to watch TV. Channel after channel, nothing but gore and violence. No wonder there was so much trouble in the world. Her thumb on the off button she watched the screen dissolve into darkness.

Change into pajamas, she admonished herself before nodding off.

She awakened, dazed, to a banging on her front door. Young male voices, unfamiliar, demanding. "Trick or treat....Give us our treats, or see our tricks." The banging continued. "We know you're in there.'

Cautiously she bent back a corner slat of the blind and peered out. A gangly youth in a ski mask was reaching down toward her chrysanthemums. She banged on the window pane, her mouth forming the words "Stop it."

"I tell you, she's a witch"; a giggling teenaged shriek. "No treats, then tricks!"

Not my chrysanthemums, she thought in panic. She stumbled into the darkened living room. Better to sacrifice the brownies than her flowers. She grabbed the basket and pulled the front door open a few inches. Her eyes fell on a tall youth, waving an uprooted chrysanthemum over his head as his companions clapped.

Her breath coming in short gasps, she set the basket atop the brick divider wall and shoved the door shut.

"Hey, old lady, we don't want no cheap sweets. We're collecting for charity."

"Yeah," another voice laughed. "Youth charity. For wayward boys." Through the peephole, she could see them retreat toward her car. She exhaled in relief. They were leaving. Thank God. And then, under the street light, she saw the flash of a spray can, orange paint streaking the side of her blue Corolla.

Still in darkness, she grabbed across the counter to the kitchen wall phone and dialed 911.

“All operators are currently busy. If this is a call to report Halloween pranksters, please leave the lines open for emergencies of physical danger. For damage to property, at the beep record your name, address and the nature of your complaint.”

Heart sinking, she complied. Outside the shrieks of glee continued.

She felt a surge of hot rage, blood pounding in her ears. She was alone, powerless. Breathe slowly, she told herself, try to think. She trembled with anger at her own helplessness. She had nothing with which to stop them. No gun, nothing….not even a canister of mace.

If only…..Frantically she felt her way over to the sink, opened the cabinet beneath. A fogger. She had a fogger, guaranteed to rid her patio of rodents, vermin. Her fingers found it behind a bottle of detergent. Unused, because the label warned it was unsafe for pets, and she hadn’t wanted to risk her neighbor’s new puppy.

Perhaps, if it fogged around her front door, it might interrupt them, drive them away before they attacked her car further, possibly slashing tires, breaking windows. But she would have to open the front door.

Through the peephole she saw them around her car, now three of them aiming spray cans of black, yellow and red. The car was at least ten feet away. Would the fogger reach that far? In desperation, she placed her forefinger on the nozzle, shoved the door open a scant three inches and thrust her hand, forefinger on the fogger’s nozzle, through the opening. As fast as she could, she pressed downward until she felt the nozzle lock into place. But in her haste to place it on the side wall, aimed at the hoodlums, the fogger fell sideways against the brownie basket. From behind her bolted door she watched in despair as the spray, initially strong, sputtered and stopped. No fog reached the hoodlums, who, admiring their destructive handiwork, never even noticed.

They stood huddled together, somewhat back from the car, seeming to lose interest. The fat one tossed an empty spray can toward the havoc of her uprooted flowers. "Hey, man," he guffawed, "the old witch got a treat coming when she sees this. He wandered over and grabbed the basket. "Hey, can't forget our treats. Ummm, brownies."

"Gimme one," the tall gangly guy reached out his hand, grabbing. Apparently hungry from their destructive exertion, they moved nonchalantly into the night, munching on her brownies.

Too numb to think, she collapsed on the sofa in exhaustion.

She awoke in the half-light of early dawn, groggy. At first she thought it had been a nightmare, until she pulled up the corner of the blind for reassurance and saw the devastation. With dread, she struggled to her feet, unbolted the door. In the cold air, she forced herself to look at her car. "Bitch-mobile" was emblazoned across its side, amid the squiggles, curlicues. She reached down to pick up a wilted, uprooted chrysanthemum, and saw the useless fogger, now fallen onto her walkway. Wearily she picked it up and made her way inside.

Perhaps she would feel better after hot tea. She set the fogger on the counter, careful not to jar it into going off again. As she did so, her eyes fell on the skull and cross bones on the can - "Warning: Poison". Squinting she tried to read the small print, then reached for her magnifying glass beside her recipe file. "If ingested, causes severe cramping, vomiting; seek immediate medical attention." Aghast, she ran her hands under the faucet, squirted antibacterial soap on them, and grabbed a paper towel to wipe the counter. She sank down onto the padded dinette bench. In a moment, she thought, she should wipe the counter and sink with bleach.

And then the realization hit her. The brownies. The fogger had sprayed directly onto the brownies. And the boys had eaten them. Surely if they felt sick they would have sense enough to go to an Emergency Room. If the Emergency Room pumped their stomachs, found the poisoned brownies, reported to the police the source… But the boys couldn't admit where they had gotten the brownies lest they be charged with damaging her car. An image of the gangly teenager, lying motionless in a ditch, flashed into her mind.

Trembling, she turned on the TV for the 7 am news, scarcely breathing as she listened for announcements of dead bodies, ER visits. The TV camera panned streets of trees twined with toilet-paper, an overpass where a scaffold held city workers painting over graffiti. An ER clip focused on a 10 year old having his hand bandaged, after he had not removed it quickly enough from a slammed door.

Back in the kitchen, she gingerly lifted the fogger. It felt empty. Heart pounding, she thrust the canister into a plastic Wal-Mart bag, already containing banana peels and discarded oatmeal of yesterday. She wiped the counter with a wet paper towel, chloroxed another towel, wiped the counter again and the sink, thrust them into regular garbage bag, tying it shut.

Heading out the door toward the dumpster, she avoided the sight of her garishly disfigured car. On her way back to the apartment, she searched for signs of brownies. There were none. She brought out her broom, carefully swept debris from the walkway back into the flower bed and smoothed down the loosened soil.

At 8 a. m. she saw the police patrol car in the parking lot, one blue-coated officer photographing her car, the other taking notes. A moment later the inevitable knock on her door. She braced herself, opened the door, almost extending her hands for the anticipated cuffs.

"Morning ma'am", he said, holding a metal clipboard thick with papers. She was relieved to see that he was middle aged. She braced herself against the door frame.

"You okay standing, or do we need to go inside where you can sit down?"

"I'm all right" she managed to murmur.

"That your car?"

She nodded.

"A shame" the officer said. "You got insurance?"

"A high deductible."

He kept writing. "Any idea who the perpetrators were?"

She shook her head.

"You get a good look at them?"

"It was dark....Mostly I just heard them, .I called 911.

"You and half the population of Leesboro. Sorry we couldn't get here sooner; gang-fight over in fourth precinct." He shook his head. "Seems like it gets worse every year."

He pulled out a carbon from the clip board he had been writing on. "Take this to your insurance agent. You might also try your homeowner's policy."

He turned to leave.

Hannah hesitated a minute. "Officer, what happens …I mean, if you catch them?"

He turned, and she could see how weary he was. "Lady, I hate to say this, but the probability is slim." He glanced down at the bulging clipboard. "I got eleven more complaints to investigate this morning. Unless someone saw them, can make an identification… Too bad. These kids need some stiff punishment, need to be taught a lesson." He walked back toward his waiting buddy in the patrol car.

When she went back inside, her phone was ringing. Jean, who, after hearing the car's condition but not Hannah's actions, went onto the computer. She called back with instructions: "Move your car to the shade, wash it. When it's dry use acetone nail polish remover to gently rub the spray paint off."

Embarrassed to drive the car, .Hanna called her pharmacy, had them send over six bottles of nail polish remover and container of Extra-strength Tylenol. The sun was out, warming her as she worked. She felt energized by having a task to do. Afterwards, the Corolla didn't look great, but then it hadn't looked very good before the spray job. Perhaps tomorrow, after she waxed it.

That evening the couple from next door came with two pots of chrysanthemums. "If we had only been here, maybe we could have stopped them."

Which would have been the end of it, except for a chance remark at church on Sunday. The pastor had chosen as his text "Forgive them, for they know not what they do". She shivered, uncertain if this meant she should forgive the marauders, or if she should be forgiven for damage she might have accidentally done to them.

Over coffee in the church parlor, she heard a neighbor from the next block, complaining to a man whose back was to her. "Forgive, hell, what some people need is a good horse whipping." Carefully she turned her good ear in his direction and listened. "Some drunks came right up on our patio, threw up all over our good porch furniture. What a mess. We couldn't even donate the pillows to the Salvation Army."

"Find out who it was?" queried the man to whom he spoke.

"Not a sign. All we found were two empty cans of spray paint." He shook his head. "If only, just once, someone would force these irresponsible jackasses to suffer the consequences."

Hannah smiled, heading toward a tray of chocolate donuts. Against her diet, but a just dessert.

CASSANDRA AND GEORGE W.

Spring 2006

They had turned off the freeway onto an old asphalt road known as “the cut-off”. Running along a narrow gorge with steep mountains on both sides, the road was a short route to Huntsville, rarely used except by local residents or truckers late with a load for the Arsenal. “Tornado Alley” the locals called it.

Cass sat tensely in the passenger seat beside her niece, Heather, who drove the white Camry. Until last year the Camry had belonged to Cass. She disliked her auburn-haired niece, but the overheated assisted living facility, where Cass must wait out her days, allowed only a relative to sign her out. For this longed-for brief trip -- a last visit to the old cottage, built 87 years ago by her long-dead grandparents. Tomorrow a woman from the Historical Society would select items of her family’s past for the county museum. On Tuesday she would meet with her lawyer to sign papers allowing a gas company to drill for methane.

The car radio, tuned to a soft rock station, sputtered, the announcer’s voice difficult to hear above the static: “George W. Bush...Birmingham...fundraiser Redstone Arsenal.” The radio crackled unintelligibly.

"This miserable radio has never worked right," Heather complained. "If I had any money, I'd buy a new one."

Cass' stomach muscles tensed at her niece's endless poor-mouthing. "We're in a ravine here," she tried to explain. "The radio signals are blocked by the hills." In the tension within the car Cass longed for a breath of fresh air. Cautiously she lowered the window.

The air felt strangely warm for early March,-warmer even than it would be in April when she would have preferred to make this visit. But her niece was traveling this weekend to serve as a volunteer for the Bush fundraiser in Huntsville. Cass had seized the opportunity, knowing that no offer would come from Heather. "I want you to take me to the cabin on your way up," she had insisted firmly, as her niece protested. "You can drop me off Friday afternoon, and pick me up Sunday on your way home."

Now, in the silence, Cass studied Heather --the burnished hair, faultless skin, surprisingly pale blue eyes. Pretty. And very eager to meet Alabama's wealthiest, who were anteing up $2000 a plate to hear their president gloat over increased war appropriations.

"Just think. Tomorrow I'll be getting to see President Bush!"

Cass clenched her teeth.

"Sometimes I think you don't care about our President."

The fresh air emboldened Cass. "I think the bastard has the moral compass of an eight-year-old school bully." She smiled at the wave energy she felt upon this expression of rage which had churned in her for so long. The look of irritation that flashed across Heather's face pleased her.*I'm not dead yet,* she thought defiantly.

As the road wound downhill into “The Hollow” Cass could see her grandparents’ home, its rock cellar built into the mountainside: a shingled cottage above the stone foundation. “Here, turn right.”

Immediately they heard dogs barking. Otto, from next door, limped toward them. He opened the car door.

“Otto, my niece, Heather. Heather, Otto. He’s taken care of the place ever since Dad died.”

After Otto unloaded her cooler, the tote bag with her clothes for the weekend, Heather was visibly impatient. “Aunt Cass, are you sure you have everything? Your cell phone?”

Cass checked inside her pocket, not for her cell phone, which would not work here, but for her pill box. Her surcease from the pain which might otherwise overwhelm her.

Inside, Otto was moving her weekend provisions into an immaculate refrigerator. “Edna put clean sheets on the bed this morning,” he assured her. “I checked to make sure the stove, the heater, the lights were ok.”

From the kitchen chair, Cass smiled up at him in gratitude.

“I got to get home before Edna leaves to baby sit. If you need anything, give us a holler. Or better still, if it’s dark, click the lights on and off.” He flicked the light switch several times. "This’ll start the dogs barking loud enough to wake the dead, and Edna and I will come running.”

Such a relief to be here, to be near people who cared about her instead of hired staff at The Oaks.

The next morning the air felt muggy; the sky overcast and ominous. Cass sat on the porch, finishing breakfast, when Otto lumbered up the steps. "Looks like a storm brewing," she commented.

Otto nodded. "Yeah. It's like I can almost smell a tornado coming. Only it ain't. Edna saw Jennie Mae in town. Said there was a tornado warning down near York. Supposed to be traveling slow, over toward Selma. We don't have to worry."

Cass thought of the cellar, safe against the side of the mountain, an early childhood refuge against any winds that ripped through the narrow valley.

Otto scratched his head. "If it was up to me instead of that weatherman, I'd guess it'd come up through Cullman, like always."

It was cooler inside the cellar. A bare electric bulb hung from the ceiling. On a narrow table Cass had placed an old flat iron and trivet, no longer needed after the cabin got electricity but saved by her thrifty grandmother. Beside them, the churn her grandpa had used to make homebrew. A box of reminders he had brought home from World War I: a rusted out pineapple hand grenade, a mess kit which had hung from his belt as he snaked telephone wires across "'no man's land'. Her grandfather had talked about being in Mainz after the Armistice, and how the doughboys had soaked their feet in German helmets like the one Cass now held. In it, samples of outdated German pfennigs and marks, made useless by inflation.

From behind a row of empty Mason jars, Cass pulled out a heavy long object wrapped in yellowed, crumbling newspaper. A long double-bladed knife, with circular clamps on the broad end. Attached with a string was a cardboard tag inscribed in her father's neat handwriting. "Japanese bayonet. Okinawa. 1945." Unlike her grandfather, her father had never talked about his time during World War II.

Cass sighed. She placed the bayonet on the table, and sat down on the old sofa against the cellar's outer wall.

She was tired. She should drag herself out of the cellar, climb the porch steps to the cabin, put on clean clothes before the woman from the Historical Society arrived. Wearily, she fished in her pocket for her pillbox, extracting two of the white tablets and swallowed them.

The overhead light bulb flickered. She reached for her flashlight, grateful for its fresh batteries. But the light came back on. Through the thick walls she could dimly hear a crackle of lightning, thunder, rain battering down. As a precaution, she moved across to the bench alongside the rock of the hollowed out mountain, which formed the back wall of the cellar. And then darkness. She flicked on the flashlight. Nothing to do but wait the storm out.

She had almost nodded off when she heard the storm roaring above. She felt grit falling from the ceiling as beams creaked and shuddered. And then the terrible stillness, followed by wind and pelting rain. She tried to think: Straight line winds, channeled into a furious onslaught by the mountains? A tornado? She knew that the storm could twist back.

She could not tell how much time had elapsed before she heard scratching on the door. Or was it the wind? She moved toward the heavy oak door. Definite clawing and whimpering, as if something were in pain. She thought of Otto's dogs. Perhaps one, terrified by the lightning, had leapt the pen's fence, was now huddled against her door. A backlash from the storm threatening at any moment now. She hesitated. What if she couldn't get the door open? What if its weight slammed her against the wall? Or if the animal were not Otto's hound, but a wild creature from the woods? And then, again, the piteous cry.

She propped the flashlight on the bench. Her feet wide apart to brace herself, Cass leaned her weight against the door and pushed. Wind and rain gushed into her face as a crouched figure shoved past. Using her last ounce of strength, she managed to pull the heavy door shut. .Exhausted she turned and beheld, in the cellar's dim light, the ferret-like face of our 43rd president, George W. Bush.

"Terrorist attack," he gasped "Call the FBI, the Air Force, and Dick Cheney."

Stunned speechless, Cass stared at the water running from his hairline down his ashen face, his soaked suit. His bare feet looked like the underside of a frog.

"Weapons of mass destruction." he panted. "Grabbed my motorcade right up off the road...." He shuddered. "Sucked me right out of my limo."

"It was a torna..."

"Call Dick Cheney." He stared at her unmoving figure. "Don't you know who I am?"

His demand rankled her. If she admitted recognizing him, then she would have to do his bidding. She hesitated. Then she heard her own words, as surprising to her as the lines from an old black and white movie, a momentarily inspired fiction. "Lemuel Musgrove. They done let you out of the drunk tank. Welcome home."

"I'm George Bush, you hillbilly ninny. Don't you watch television?"

It really was him, not just the TV image at which she mouthed expletives during the evening news. He believed her outlandish ruse. She blinked in astonishment. George W at her mercy. Reckless, forsaking judgment or restraint, she plunged ahead. “Shush, Lemuel, you don’t want anyone thinking you’re George Bush. I know you and him are both drunks. And you had trouble learning in school just like him.” With heady delight, she watched the red flush rise up George W’s neck. “But George Bush is a murderer, and you, Lemuel, thank God, are not.”

GW narrowed his eyes, shifting his head in a familiar sideways gaze. “You believe in God, granny?”

Not your God, Cass thought in silence, waiting.

“Well, God sent me to save this country.” He paused, with what she supposed he thought a charming smile. “Now for God’s sake, call Dick Cheney.”

Cass smiled back in giddy triumph. “Get hold of yourself, Lemuel. You know as well as me how all them church people is always looking over their shoulders for the devil. Seems they found and elected him.”

Weakly insistent, repeating it like a mantra to convince himself. “I am George Bush, President of the United States.”

A peal of thunder reverberated through the shadowy cellar. Cass found the bench behind her and sank down onto it. Here was George W, whose advisors were too cowardly to confront him with the truth. Cass took a deep breath. George W. slumped on an old sofa across from her. Maybe, just maybe, if he heard the truth this once, if he had to listen…

She recalled a tactic she had used with her more ornery, less apt students. “Look here, Lemuel. I want you to sit there quietly, and think about all those boys George W. Bush has gotten killed, shot, or just plain driven crazy by what they were made to do.” She held her voice even, almost hypnotic. "Then I want you to think about all those poor women and children, getting bombed to death."

"Co-lat-y-ral damage. Rummy told me."

"And those young Muslim guys, willing to blow themselves up to get us out of their country."

GWB opened his mouth to protest.

Again Cass shushed him. "Keep thinking about the thousands of human beings he's caused to die. Lying, killing people, trying to prove he's right, when he's not." Rage surged in her veins. "And then you tell me, Lemuel, if you'd still be proud for people to think you're George W." Spent, she rested her back against the bench.

She heard an ominous roar from outside, the storm was starting up again. In horror she watched a wooden beam tilt: The beam supported an iron brace directly above George W's head. Automatically she warned: "Move over here, against this wall."

A tremendous crackle of lightning; the shelves holding empty mason jars collapsed forward between Cass and the crouching figure on the couch. Shards of glass splintered over the hard earthen floor.

"You need to crawl over that mess and get over here by the mountain where it's safe."

George W peered at the broken glass, wriggled his bare toes, and looked back at her in childlike fury. "What are you trying to pull on me?"

Against her back Cass felt the boards of the bench shift, the boards which extended to the corner post, holding it in place. The post tilted forward more precariously, the iron brace it supported wobbled unevenly. If it fell, the world would no longer have to contend with George W.

She did not want him to die casually; she wanted him to face an International Court for Crimes Against Humanity.

Cass jammed her feet against the floor. With all her might she wedged herself hard against the low board on the back of the bench. She felt the boards steady; watched the post stop moving forward. Her breath came in short gasps. She was not certain how long she could hold on. She could simply let go, and...

She felt a draft of wind, glimpsed daylight coming through a crack now open in the wall to the right of George W's head. The storm was dying down. She waited, straining.

And then Otto's dogs barking furiously. The rush of feet...A loud voice "Secure perimeters," as if from a bullhorn. Finally, help was here.

Three shots, and the barking ceased.

"President Bush," the bullhorn sounded, "Are you in there? Our devices indicate your presence." Through the crack in the wall a small microphone descended. "Are you alive? Can you hear us?"

A feeble gasp from George W. "Terrorists."

"You're being held by terrorists....a hostage?"

"Weapons of mass destruction."

"Hang on, sir. We'll get you out."

The sound of a monster motor being revved up, a crash against the cellar door, wood splintering. Helmeted men shoved past her, boots crushing the glass shards as they leaped across the downed shelves to the shaking figure of George W.

Abruptly Cass felt herself hurled groundward, wrists pinned behind her back. As she was dragged toward daylight, marauding hands pulled the pillbox from her pocket.

A heavily gloved hand reached out. Grasping the pillbox. Slowly the visored man in a thickly padded hazmat suit pulled it open. "Anthrax," he shouted. "Secure with all necessary precautions."

In her dizzy nausea Cass tried to explain. "Oxycontin." And then she passed out.

When she came to, Cass found herself strapped to a gurney, shivering in her damp clothes. Above her, she could hear the whir of helicopter blades. Below she glimpsed the freeway: bumper to bumper with humvees, TV vehicles, black limousines with VIP flags on their antennae, MPs setting out orange traffic cones. All heading toward the cutoff.

Her gurney was propped at an angle behind the pilots' seats. "Where are you taking me?"

No response from the helmeted pilots.

Nausea threatened her. Press cars. From inside her pain-wracked, dimming world, Cass wondered if there might be reporters when she was delivered to her unknown destination. She tensed, struggling to think what she might say, how to tell them…She strained to hang onto consciousness, hang onto the hope that some reporter might listen, might believe what she had to say…

People could hang on so long as they had a purpose. Teeth chattering, she thought of the soldiers in Iraq, whose families must hang onto some belief that their deaths, their wounds, their disrupted lives and battered psyches had some purpose, because they could not bear the reality otherwise. And the terrible advantage of this to George W.

"Hey, buddy" she heard one of the pilots mutter, "I bet we're on the news right now. You still got that radio in your gear?"

Cass felt the seat against which her gurney was propped push back slightly; the co-pilot must be leaning forward.

And then through her darkened mist, the resonant voice of a news commentator:

"We repeat: your president is safe. A vast terrorist plot has been foiled. I have beside me Vice President Cheney with details of this viciously attempted crime."

"Dick Cheney here. At 1:47 Eastern Standard time President George W Bush was abducted and held hostage in a mountain bunker in North Alabama. With the same courage and decisiveness he displayed during the 911 attacks, your president had left the safety of his motorcade to rescue an elderly demented woman from a raging storm. This woman was a decoy for a massive network of co-conspirators, who then held our Commander-in-Chief hostage until his rescue by US Special Forces. FBI officials report finding a large cache of foreign weapons and currency in the terrorists' mountainside lair."

A babble of voices in the background, and then the commentator. "Karl Rove is speaking to the media now:"

"Your government will use all resources of this great democracy to seek out and destroy these terrorists whose very existence threatens us all."

A voice emerging from the cacophony "Have you captured any of the conspirators? What about the old lady?"

"She is currently being airlifted by medevac to a renowned medical center, to be treated for massive injuries inflicted by the storm."

From her tenaciously held consciousness, Cass's mind protested. *The storm didn't injure me…*

A shout "When can we interview her?"

A jumble of voices, a long pause, and again the announcer. "I have just been handed a bulletin. Seven minutes ago the female terrorist expired during flight. We repeat: at 3:19 Eastern Standard Time, the female conspirator has been confirmed dead."

Vaguely heard in the background, sounds of the Stars Spangled Banner, and the commentator intoning: "Let us now offer up prayers of thanksgiving for the miraculous salvation of our beloved president, George W. Bush."

HOW CANCER SAVED MY LIFE

Will I live, or merely linger,
In a morphine mist…?

Lines written June 2000
after surgery for breast cancer

It was a spring too beautiful to bear. Azaleas, dogwood, flowering crabapple bloomed in the yard of my small hilltop home; at my door, the fragrance of gardenias.

I went with two friends to hear Alabama writers read their works, then across the street to an art exhibition in the park. Listening to good jazz, we ate Greek food. I was aware of being happy for the first time in months.

Three weeks earlier my mother had died at age 101. We had had a difficult relationship. She, beautiful and charming, had deplored the social ineptitude of her spoiled only child. At her death I wept, not for her but for myself, for the loss of any possibility that I might someday hear the longed for words, that I was a decent human being.

The next week I sat in my living room, computing taxes on her estate, uncertain if she might have made a last-minute will leaving everything to the handsome nephew of my late father. The nephew, upon whom she doted, had often barged into town and into her nursing home room, smug in his anticipation of her bequest, critical and contemptuous of my daily struggles to comfort her and to obtain the care she needed.

Now, around me were her priceless antiques, boxes of her belonging stacked against the wall. A mile away was a rented storage locker crammed full of possessions she could not relinquish.

As a reward for what I anticipated would be my summer's task of getting her estate and my own life in order, I made reservations with Elderhostel for a trip to India in the fall.

And then, CANCER. The casual, accidental discovery. My excellent physician initially reassured me that my mammogram six months earlier had been clear and sent me for further tests. When the results came back she ran, not walked, across the hall to the office of a surgeon specializing in breast cancer.

The morning after my radical mastectomy I awoke to an epiphany: my mother was no longer here to demand what I had done wrong to cause this, nor to charm my doctors to do her bidding. My kind father could no longer admonish me that I was upsetting his beloved wife. Suddenly I felt light and free.

An hour later the surgeon parried my questions until I pinned her down. "Seven nodes, aggressive," she murmured, babbling on about the benefits of tamoxifen.

From my years heading the Health/Mental Health curriculum in a graduate School of Social Work, I knew the grim statistics.

But I can't die, I thought. *I can't die and leave everything such a mess.* Never for a moment did I doubt that I would be having chemo and radiation because that would be my best chance for survival.

What I did not know then was that only 8% of women over 65 with breast cancer received chemotherapy because physicians believed that the "many miserable side effects of chemo were too much of an assault on elderly bodies". When I read this in 2002 I wanted scream in rage: *Do you just plan to let them die?* At that moment I resolved to someday write this article, to say to newly diagnosed women as frightened as I was: *You* ***can*** *get through this and get your life back. Perhaps an even better life.*

Now, eleven years later, I know that every patient's experience is unique. Treatments change, but the terror remains.

The oncologist to whom I was referred had a reputation for being hard-nosed, confronting his patients with the realities of their prognoses.

Dutifully I took a friend with me to the initial appointment. Stunned, I heard her request that he not give me any medications which might cause me to lose my hair. *My God*, I thought, *my life is at stake. Who gives a dam about my hair, which frequently looks like hell anyway.*

At the end of the interview for the first time he looked me straight on. "I can cure you."

I didn't believe him.

He then asked if I would be willing to participate in a research study: clinical trials of massive doses of paclitaxol and other cancer medications. I knew nothing about cancer medications, but his mention of research was, after my years in academia, like a homecoming.

On the way from his office I paused by the doorway of the chemo lab and stared. Rows of patients in recliners: young women who looked healthy, men with shaved heads, middle-aged women reading, ashen-faced patients slumped over, sleeping. Beside each a pole from which hung a plastic bag of fluid, with tubes running down to each patient. I took a deep breath in determination: *If they could do it, so could I.*

Back home alone, I took stock. I was 71, retired, long ago divorced with no children. My only relatives were the resentful cousins. For more than thirty years I had lived alone, in evening retreat from the daily abrasion of human relationships: the power struggles of academia, the pressure of preparing lectures and responding to the needs of students and patients.

During those last exhausting years of my mother's life, my friends had been great. But they had done enough. I could not expect more.

Financially secure, emotionally I was running on empty.

I was operating at three levels. Cognitively I knew I had to make plans, get myself into a facility where, as I became more ill, I would be cared for.

But on a deeper, childlike level, I never really believed I was going to die. And, waking in moments of midnight darkness, I shoved back down into my most irrational depths the thought that this cancer was retribution for not making my mother happy. Or perhaps having cancer might assuage my guilt, a penance that might at last set me free.

Friends called, inviting me to lunch. How do you say, to a casual, unsuspecting caller: "*I have cancer? I'm scared I might die*"? I feared that if they heard my desperation they might back off, uncomfortable at my neediness, cautious about what might be demanded of them. I needed them too much to risk loss of these fragile human contacts. I said nothing.

From Philadelphia a phone call from the husband of an old friend who had died of lung cancer. In the early 1950's Sally and I had been in Foreign Service together, stationed in beautiful Bad Godesberg, Germany. From our offices overlooking the Rhine, weekdays we typed for Harvard lawyers and economists the Contractual Agreements upon which the German economic recovery was based. Weekends we travelled.

Back in the US after their marriage, we visited frequently. In the mid-90's, when Sally was diagnosed with lung cancer, I watched in heartbreak but admiration as she bravely prepared her children and grandchildren for her death. Now I blurted out my own fears.

He did not hesitate. "You're coming to Philadelphia. Stay with Kris and me. We can get you the best specialists."

Blinking back tears, I protested. I didn't even know his new wife, only that she, too, had been widowed by cancer. I couldn't put them under such stress. Finally I countered: "I'm going to M. D. Anderson in Houston." It was the only facility that might trump the hospital he had just recommended.

The moment I said it, I knew that I didn't want to leave Birmingham, didn't want to face chemo alone in a motel room in a strange city. I wanted to stay in the city where I was born.

If I walked across the street from my home and gazed downhill along a power-line cut through, I could see the rooftops of St. Martins, an Episcopal Retirement Center. Across the street from their spacious grounds was the mall where I shopped, my bank, a branch library, the station which serviced my car.

When I drove through St. Martin's grilled iron entry gates, past the rose garden and the stately trees, I could look up at balconies bright with hanging baskets. At the entrance to the residential apartments, a covered walkway led to the Assisted Living facility; beyond that a nursing home.

Inside, parquet floors and oriental rugs. In the great room, residents sat in groups on cheerful chintz floral sofas; they looked relaxed. There was an aura of well-being.

The administrator took me on a tour: .past the library with floor to ceiling bookshelves, a table full of the latest magazines, a computer. Past the small chapel, and into a sunny, flower-filled dining room.

I admired the administrator's skill in interviewing me, her openness in answering my questions. Yes, they anticipated a vacancy within two months for a large one bedroom unit whose balcony overlooked the courtyard. I filled out the extensive application form that afternoon, and the next morning, one week after my mastectomy, I was on the waiting list.

During the following days, on my way home from lab procedures necessary before I began chemotherapy, I would drive through the beautiful grounds of St. Martins to comfort myself.

Chemo. I remembered a friend who had been so sick from treatments that she began vomiting the moment she got into the car for her husband to drive her to appointments. My hands clenched as I resolved to do whatever I had to do, terrified that I might not be able to.

When I think back on those months of chemo, what I remember most was the unfailing kindness of the nurses. While I sat tethered to an IV pole, for four hours watching the slow drip of chemicals from that suspended plastic bag toward the port in my chest, I observed them. In heavy leaded aprons they hurried from one patient to another, bringing a requested pillow, a blanket, a touch of reassurance. They never showed annoyance, never complained about how tired they must be. Never back-biting among themselves, they were always responsive, caring. I was in awe.

The dreaded nausea never occurred. In a fortunate fit between medication and genetic endowment, my body responded to the toxic chemicals as if they were vitamins. I was ravenous. Nurses scurried to bring me peanut butter and crackers before I dozed off. I awakened woozy, grateful that someone was driving me home.

The next morning I was queasy. Determinedly I ate peanut butter toast.. A friend called, inviting me to supper at her country home. She was a marvelous cook who spoiled guests with an array of fresh vegetables, homemade rolls and cobblers. "Don't fix much," I warned her. I'm on chemo."

Luckily she didn't take my advice. I ate like a pig, and afterwards slept like a lamb. Throughout the twelve sessions of chemo I only missed one meal. Not from nausea; I simply slept through dinner.

The side effect I hadn't anticipated was severe peripheral neuropathy, as chemical toxins damaged nerve transmission in both my feet and hands. It began slowly, a tingling numbness, ever worsening, and despite the numbness, painful.

In the office of the radiation oncologist I sat huddled in a washed out hospital gown tied with string. I couldn't even shower lest I wash away the blue dye which marked the area where a huge x-ray machine should aim its deadly beam.

Before me, my radiation oncologist stood in high heels, a red suit, looking like a size 2 fashion model from the cover of Vogue.

"My feet are numb; I can scarcely feel the gas pedal in my car," I complained, expecting some magic pill. (There's no treatment for peripheral neuropathy, but I didn't know it then.)

"You have to stop driving," she ordered firmly.

I stared at her in amazement. For me, driving was like breathing.

She was adamant. "No driving."

I complied. At least I no longer drove to radiation appointments. My remarkable network of former students went into action. A social work colleague took me to purchase a four-wheel walker (rare back in 2001) and located a shop to install hand controls for my car. Before I could get them installed, I realized that somehow, despite the numbness in my feet, I could sense the amount of pressure I was exerting on the gas pedal, the brakes. Now, eleven years later with no accidents, I'm still driving. Very cautiously!

The peripheral neuropathy seemed a small price to pay for continuing to live; I'd never dreamed of becoming a ballerina. My four-wheel walker seems like an extension of my own anatomy, as, bracing on it, I hurry down hospital corridors, stroll paths of the Botanical Gardens, rest on its seat, or haul grocery bags on it.

Midway between my second and third chemo treatments, I packed seventeen boxes of my mother's antiques and followed a moving van down the hill to St. Martins.

On that first day I stood hesitantly aside in the dining room, knowing no one, uncertain at which table I might sit. I

felt my tight new wig crawling up my scalp. With both hands holding a loaded lunch tray, I couldn't pull it back down. What if it flew off into someone's soup?

And then a gentle voice at my elbow. "Would you like to sit with us?"

There were three of them, all in their late 90's. During the weeks that followed they gently, kindly, tactfully wove around me a web of support which restored my starving soul. "We're going to get you well," promised Martha, as she cooked for me the tender young turnip greens Ruth had grown in the residents' garden.

Research has never been able to quantify the role that nurturing relationships might have in calming a patient's raging anatomy. But at St. Martins I was unbelievably happy, physical discomforts overshadowed by the joy of my days.

Afternoons I would sit curled up on a sofa in the great room, listening to a resident play the large pipe organ he had brought with him to St. Martins. I remembered the hassles back at my lake home when I had to juggle plumbers, roofers, lawn people, with a heavy teaching schedule. If only I could have lived then in a place like this.

Of course there were a few less benevolent individuals around, whom I avoided. (One does not survive 25 years of academic politics without a few skills for dealing with bastards!)

At 8 a.m. a few weeks after my move, my bedside phone rang. Probably my friend, Horty, complaining that her computer wouldn't work. Or some prerecorded exhortation to vote for a politician I detested.

An unrecognized voice on the line: "This is Ralph."

I didn't know any Ralph. I hedged, cautiously asking him to help refresh my memory of who he was.

"I'm the guy you winked at yesterday."

I never wink. Something must have been in my eye.

"I'm the one in the red baseball cap."

A hazy memory of a resident in a red baseball cap.

"I want to take you out to dinner and drinks tonight."

I tried to be polite. "That's very nice, but I can't drink. Perhaps instead we could have coffee downstairs here."

"I don't like coffee."

After I extricated myself from the conversation, I felt guilty. After all, here was someone nice enough to ask me out. I hadn't been asked out by a male in eons.

The next morning, as I made my way across the great room, past residents with their morning newspapers, I saw him, in the red baseball cap. Tentatively I approached.

He wasted no time. "Do you believe in the Bible?
"

"Mmmm...sort of." I wondered what he was getting at.

"You believe in the ten commandments?"

Another cautious "Mmmmm….."

"You know that commandment: Thou shalt not commit adultery?"

No response.

"Well, my wife is dead and you're divorced, so it wouldn't be adultery."

Aghast, I sought the shortest route out of the room. Cancer to the rescue. "I'm too sick for this," I gasped and fled. I didn't even dare to *think* about sex these days: it might stimulate my estrogen-fed cancer!

Outside in the parking lot I recognized the source of my irresistible charm: I could still drive!

Mostly I felt OK physically. But at times of exhaustion, and in moments of midnight malaise, I soothed myself: *Just keep breathing and you'll get through this.*

With the pale specter of life's limits always hovering, I did those things I had always longed to do. I self-published a collection of short stories. I bought for the rose garden a dark wood gazebo where residents could sit and read. Alongside it a water-fountain for those gardening, or out for a stroll. Around the base of the gazebo we planted hibiscus, mandevilla, lilies. Residents hung gaskets of pink impatiens, begonias, and ivy to trail from its arches.

Friends, former students and colleagues visited often, at first out of duty. Later, reassured that I was well-cared for, they returned to enjoy with me the musicals, lectures and picnics the dedicated staff arranged.

During the next year, at meetings of a support group for breast cancer patients, I grew ever more aware of how cancer ravages not only the body but the relationships in which patients spend their everyday lives.

The dilemma in all human relationships is how to sustain the connectedness we crave, yet preserve our own boundaries. How not get taken over, to be used as a pawn in another's unacknowledged internal scripts.

Cancer disrupts the subtle power balance of reciprocal relationships. While family members and friends are often eager, at least at first, to provide help and encouragement, often they, in caring desperation (or sometimes pure narcissism) often take over and demand that the patient do what they deem best. With dismay I watched patients, guilty for the burden their illness might impose, valiantly use their meager emotional energy to allay the anxiety of others. Sadly I saw them sacrifice their own desires and self direction to accede to demands frequently not in their best interest. *The task of those who care about the patient is to control their own anxiety, not, out of their anxiety, to try to control the patient.*

This dilemma is further complicated by the power imbalances between medical staff, caregivers, and the patient, who all-too-often finds herself at the bottom of the hierarchical totem pole.

I was grateful for my own good fortune during those three years at St. Martins. The kindness of residents and staff made this time of my recovery more pleasant than I had any right to hope for. But I also knew that even without these conveniences of care, of creature comforts, I would have resolutely put one foot in front of the other and marched through the days. Because what else can one do?

By late 2003, dismayed by staff changes and concerned that I might soon be incapacitated by peripheral neuropathy, I moved from St. Martins to a suburban Assisted Living facility. Run by an out-of-state corporation, Eldercrest (not its real name) was built to accommodate the mobility impaired.

For those cancer patients who hope to get their needs met by moving to a retirement center, two strong caveats:

Admission to such facilities can be extremely expensive. One must "purchase" her living unit, as well as pay high monthly fees. After admission, if a resident wishes to move, either because her condition changes or she is unhappy, she may face huge financial penalties.

Moving from one's private home into group living can be stressful. In return for the expected care, one must relinquish a great deal of control over decisions in one's life. Even in the best facilities there is always some tension between needs of the resident, and those of the staff. In less well run establishments, such disparity can become unpleasant. At worst the vulnerable patient becomes a faceless commodity at the mercy of uncaring staff, used for the convenience of administrators and profit for the corporation.

Initially Eldercrest was managed by a remarkable Director who knew both how to reassure elderly patients and keep the place running smoothly. When he later left for a well-deserved better job, several excellent staff members also departed.

The corporation hired a woman who was both incompetent and overwhelmed. Rules replaced reason. In medical emergencies (which so often occur at night) the resident was not permitted to call 911. Instead his request must be filtered through a poorly trained nursing attendant who knew far less about the resident's illness than the resident himself.

Residents died, whisked off at midnight as we peered from our windows down on the flashing red lights of emergency vehicles. The next morning staff would not respond to questions about the resident. No announcement about the funeral; no sympathy cards for us to sign. Nothing.

Organizational structure crumbled. Nursing assistants wandered off to gossip, leaving their wheel-chair patients to wait alone. Aides barged into the rooms of infirm patients, lolling around to watch TV as they hid out from any summons to other duties. The weak, sick elderly feared that unless they appeased the aides, they would receive even worse care.

On one cold weekend, with pipes bursting and residents complaining, the harried maintenance man telephoned the administrator, requesting authorization to call a plumber. It was refused. Enraged, he stacked his tools on a chair with a large sign, "I quit", and left. The temporary weekend receptionist ran from apartment to apartment with a toilet plunger, trying to preserve sanitation.

Corporate fired half the staff. Unfortunately the wrong half. Managers, directors, specialists came and went so frequently nobody knew who was in charge.

Residents grew irritable, bickering among themselves. At every meal one vicious tablemate demanded to see the head of dietary (one of the few competent people remaining) and angrily berated her. Another tablemate, annoyed at the cigarette butts on the pathway of her morning walk, collected and placed these butts (without benefit of a plastic bag), on our breakfast table. In a late-life resurgence of testosterone, one aged male raced his electric scooter down the halls as residents plastered themselves against the wall. When he ran over and injured the feet of one docile soul, he was not even reprimanded.

Every night the sleep of residents was pierced by shrills of a short-circuited fire alarm which none of the few night staff knew how to turn off. An even worse assault on our eardrums occurred in the dining room. The new Activities Director turned up the "background music" to ear-splitting decibels as she cavorted around the room like an arthritic cow. When an elderly gentleman, his frail wife cringing at his side, pleaded with her to turn down the volume down, she haughtily refused.

I, who had long taught students to observe "who does what to whom" in dysfunctional families and organizations, was appalled. Had this been a Saturday Night Live satire, it would have been deemed too "over the top" to use. In a building full of elderly, impaired people, striving to make the best of difficult conditions, it was a tragedy.

February 2005

From the chaos of Eldercrest, I drove ten miles to the Camellia Show at the Birmingham Botanical Gardens. Drove past the familiar shops of Mountain Brook: post office, bank, a favorite restaurant. A few blocks away the house where my parents had lived for forty-three years, where I had grown up. Along Lane Park Road, to my left the Gardens, on my right the beautifully landscaped grounds of stately garden apartments. Apartments where my friends had lived during the early years of their marriages, and to which their parents had later downsized. Townhomes where my parents, upon my return from Philadelphia forty years ago, had wanted me to live. I felt a wave of homesickness, of longing for the lost possibility of ever living there.

But was the possibility really past for me?

I was 76 years old, on a walker, the shadow of a cancer recurrence always hovering. Could I risk another move? If not now, when?

An acquaintance who had tried to boss me since childhood harangued me: I was a fool to consider this.

A month later on an early spring morning, I drove behind the moving van under a canopy of white pear blossoms, past young people jogging, retirees walking their dogs. Squirrels scampered across green lawns bordered by pansies, jonquils, and early tulips. Birds sang. I was home.

October 2011

On a crisp autumn morning I sit at a table on the sun-dappled back lawn of my townhome. The yard is a wide expanse of freshly mowed green, cupped by a ring of tall trees rising against a cloud-streaked blue sky. At the far end, two giant magnolias stand before a fence; just beyond it, a brook and golf course. Across from this apartment complex, the Botanical Gardens await an afternoon stroll. If I drive past the entrance to the Gardens, follow the road along the golf course, I am soon at the Mountain Brook library.

On the table before me is my laptop, rich with emails from friends from every era of my life. On days less inviting, I can sit in my front bedroom, looking out over park-like grounds, and browse the world. The librarian has programmed my computer so that I can download books without leaving my bed. But I seldom remain late in bed. Friends beckon me futureward into a world too fascinating to relinquish.

For ten years my lab reports have revealed no markers of cancer. I am no longer on Aromasin. But always the shadow: what if a single errant cell might have eluded the toxic chemicals, the bombardment of radiation, and lurk unseen; remission ended?

The gift of cancer to me was this: faced with the reality that I might no longer exist, the unimportant fell away like chaff winnowed in the wind. Every day a gift, touched by unexpected kindness, astounded by small delights.

I recognize that my own undeserved good fortune has been the result of luck, shaped by evolution, genetic endowment, and cultural heritage. Sadly the world is not fair. I see the wan and worried faces of Wal-Mart shoppers; observe on nightly news the chaos of a planet overpopulated by careless copulation. People of principle and bravery suffer and die needlessly. This tale of my own fortunate pathway through cancer is scarcely relevant compared with the experience of those admired individuals who struggle against much harsher realities. But it is all I have to offer. And still I sing inside.

Thirty years ago a favorite student, upon graduation, presented me with a sampler she had embroidered. At the time I recognized that its message reflected her compassionate outlook rather than my own. However, since it has hung on my living room wall, visitors have assumed it represents my beliefs and I have aspired to grow toward it. Today I recognize that it voices the philosophy of so many cancer patients:

I shall pass this way but once
Therefore any good that I can do
Or any kindness I can show
Let me do it now
For I shall not pass this way again.

Attributed to Stephen Grelet
(1773-1855)

HAVE A HAPPY JOURNEY

CPSIA information can be obtained at www.ICGtesting.com
Printed in the USA
LVOW042304131111

254759LV00001B/6/P

9 781600 476594